"Do I get one of those hugs?"

"Of course you do." She tried to sou~~nd~~ ...
but her heart thumped as ~~h~~ ...
set gray ones. Th ...
She stepped clos ...
around her waist ...
up, knowing her ... ~~Th~~ank
you for helping m ...

She went up on her toes and brushed a quick, feathery kiss on his cheek. Then she pulled out of his embrace.

A nervous little laugh escaped her as she suddenly remembered the roomful of people. Thankfully she held her feet to the floor long enough to carry her to a chair.

As she listened to the singing, Jolene's heart sang for joy. She loved this time with family and friends in their home, and especially loved that Riley was among them. The glances he sent her way every few minutes made her heart flutter. A vision grew in her mind of doing this every year.

Lord, don't let me dream this way if it's impossible. Riley's special to me. Please draw him to You.

Books by Helen Gray

Love Inspired Heartsong Presents

Ozark Sweetheart
Ozark Reunion

HELEN GRAY

grew up in a small Missouri town and married her pastor. They have three grown children. If her writing touches others in even a small way, she considers it a blessing and thanks God for the opportunity.

HELEN GRAY

Ozark Reunion

HEARTSONG
PRESENTS

Recycling programs
for this product may
not exist in your area.

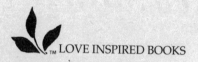

LOVE INSPIRED BOOKS

ISBN-13: 978-0-373-48713-4

OZARK REUNION

Copyright © 2014 by Helen Gray

www.Harlequin.com

Printed in U.S.A.

Hear instruction, and be wise, and refuse it not.
—*Proverbs* 8:33

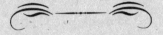

Many thanks to my number one support group—
Ken, Ginger and John, Derek, and Deven—
my wonderful and patient family. I am humbled
by your neverending love and belief in me.

And thank You, God,
for granting my long sought dream.

Chapter 1

Riley Blake tramped through the trees, a rifle cradled in one arm, the other hand clutching a stick from which two dead squirrels dangled. No longer walking with hunter stealth, dead leaves rustled beneath his feet.

He emerged from the woods near the road and worked his way through the strands of a barbed-wire fence. As he stood upright and pulled his coat tighter against the cold November air, a movement to his left drew his attention. The late-afternoon sun highlighted a figure in a dress flying down the hill toward him on a bicycle.

He recognized Jolene Delaney's little sister, Irene. A pretty black-haired thing, she had been a familiar sight riding up and down this road from the time she could ride a bike. Riley guessed she would be about fifteen now. But the way she was bent low and pedaling furiously signaled trouble.

Alarm skittered up his spine. Could something have happened to Jolene? Not that she mattered to him in any special way. Not anymore. He hopped across the ditch and waited by the gravel road.

The girl braked and skidded to a stop a few feet past him, hopped off and backed up. "Dad cut his leg with the ax. Bad," she added, struggling to draw air into her lungs. She looked pale and scared. She must have beaten all her speed records on the mile ride from her house.

"Let's get Mom. She'll know what to do."

He set out at a fast clip for the house a hundred yards farther down the road. Irene pushed her bike alongside him. "When did it happen?" he asked, the squirrels flopping against his knee.

"Sometime…this afternoon," she managed to say between gasps. "I came home from school and found him on the kitchen floor. He had dragged himself in there and wrapped a towel around his leg."

"Where's Jolene?"

"She…got home right after…I did. He wouldn't…let us get a doctor."

"Do they know you're here?"

She looked over at him as they turned into the yard. "No. Dad was worried about the chores. I told him I'd do 'em." She leaned the bike against a tree.

Riley nodded and opened the front door of the small-frame structure of weathered wood. "So they think you're at the barn."

She bobbed her head in quick jerks and followed him inside the living room.

"Mom, you here?" he yelled.

His mother appeared in the kitchen door, wiping her

hands on the bib apron that draped her thin torso. Her deep blue eyes widened when they landed on Irene. "What's a matter, child?"

As Irene explained about her dad, Riley considered the fastest way to get to the Delaney house. There was no gas in the old car—no money to buy any—plus it had a flat tire. Shucks, they didn't have money for anything these days.

"I'll hitch the team to the buckboard while you get ready," he said, knowing without a doubt his mom would go to help the neighbors. Dad had gone to town on horseback to get a part for the tractor, giving Riley a couple hours off work to hunt squirrels for their supper. Trouble with the machinery was the last thing they needed.

"Have a seat and catch your breath. I'll be back in two shakes." His mom hurried to the back door and stuck her head out. "Clem," she yelled, "come finish fixin' supper. I have to leave."

Riley stepped into the kitchen and tossed the squirrels on the table on his way out the back door. Halfway to the barn he met his youngest sister, Clementine, headed to the house from the woodpile. It took him several minutes to round up the horses from the corral and harness them to the wagon. He was thankful they were in the corral rather than in the pasture across the road, where they ran free when not in use.

On his way back to the house, his mom and Irene emerged and came to meet him. He took his mom's bag and gave her a boost up onto the wagon seat. Then he tossed the bag onto her lap and ran around to climb up beside her.

"Come up here by me," his mom called over her shoulder when the girl shoved her bike up into the wagon and started to climb into the back with it. Riley clicked to the horses and set off while they were still getting settled.

Their faces were red from the cold by the time they got to the Delaney farm. He hitched the team in front of the porch that stretched across the front and wrapped around one corner of the two-story house. His mom went inside. When Irene headed for the barn, he grabbed her arm. "Go on inside with Mom. I'll do your chores."

"Thank you." She rubbed the back of a hand over her eyes and did as he said.

He started to take off, but hesitated. He needed milk buckets, and they had to be inside the house. Where Jolene was bound to be.

Well, so what. His younger sister's best friend, Miss Holier-Than-Thou, wasn't the issue here. It was her injured dad.

The Delaneys had always had a nicer house and more money than the Blakes until things got so desperate for everybody. Like so many farmers, Sam Delaney had lost his savings when the banks closed, and then the drought had forced him to sell his cattle at a loss, even slaughter some of them. He was a good man, but now he was as poor as everyone else.

As Riley's mom disappeared inside the house, the door started to close then opened again. Framed in the doorway, Jolene stood, looking as beautiful as...no, more so... than ever.

Riley's heart almost forgot to beat, numbed by the sight. She was still slender, with big brown eyes that glinted under dark brows, her long wheat-colored hair pulled back from her oval face. Five more years of maturity had only made her more beautiful than she had been as a teen.

She didn't look overjoyed to see him. Well, the feeling was mutual.

He opened his mouth to speak. Closed it. Cleared his throat and tried again. "I…uh…it's nice to see you again." The words came out thick and unnatural as his thoughts rattled around in his brain.

"I'm…fine," she said, a hand moving to her mouth in a nervous gesture. She seemed as shocked as he at their meeting.

Seconds passed, during which silent messages of anger—remembrances—passed between them.

"You look good," he said, his lips releasing his thoughts without any conscious planning on his part.

Pink colored her face. "Thank you," she said softly.

He'd taken care to avoid her for years. Now he stood here like a lightning-struck idiot. He squared his shoulders. "I hope your dad is all right."

Concern instantly clouded her features.

"We…appreciate you coming…and bringing your mother," she said, seeming to squeeze out the words.

He closed his eyes for a moment and fought for control. When he opened them, he managed to focus on the present. "Got a couple of milk buckets I can use?"

She hesitated, as if struggling to think. "I'll get them," she finally said. She turned and disappeared, and then reappeared moments later with a pail in each hand.

He stepped near the doorway and reached for them. Their hands brushed, causing both of them to flinch and complete the transfer quickly as he wrapped his fingers around the pails. "I'll feed the animals."

Regret ate at Jolene as Riley strode toward the barn, his back ramrod straight. Why had she managed to alienate him?

Her breathing was labored, her ability to think halted. She wanted to go after him, to try to make it right. With a sigh she closed the door. She didn't have time to make it right. Even if she did, she didn't know how.

Irene turned from stoking the fire in the kitchen stove. "Sorry I ducked out on chores."

Jolene nodded, her mouth locked in a tight line. "It's okay. You were scared. So am I. I'm glad you went for help."

Her sister winced. "Even if Riley came?"

"Yeah, even if Riley came," she said as she fought the memories stirred by his arrival. "Dad didn't leave you any choice about not getting the doctor."

So Irene had taken the next best action. Her little sister had grown up way too fast since their mother's death five years ago. Jolene had never minded being left with the responsibility of raising her then ten-year-old sister and taking her mother's place as the woman of the house. She had accepted that it meant not being free to marry like her girlfriends had done. But having Irene beginning to make decisions was a welcome lightening of her load.

"I'll invite Riley and his mother to supper." Irene's statement held a question.

Jolene sighed. "It's the right thing to do." Even if they wouldn't stay. Riley wouldn't, anyhow.

Back in her dad's bedroom, Jolene watched Dessie Blake check his leg and remove the bandage that Jolene had wrapped from below the knee almost to the foot. "I cleaned it good and soaked it in coal oil like he ordered," Jolene explained.

Dessie didn't look up. "You done good, Jolene. But I think we better stitch on it. I'll get a needle and thread sterilized."

Her dad glared up at them through eyes glazed with

pain. "Don't need you gals fussin' over me. I'll be fine. I have to be." He moved to rise up in the bed.

Dessie put her hand on his chest and pressed him back onto the mattress. "Sam Delaney, you use some 'a the good sense the Lord give ya and stay off that leg. That's a real nasty gash. It looks like it went clean to the bone. If ya take off on it too soon, you'll end up makin' it worse, maybe even lose the leg."

He glared like he was set to argue, but then he looked back and forth between Dessie and Jolene and eased back onto the bed.

"Riley's taking care of the chores," Dessie informed him. "So don't you worry none about anything."

Jolene exhaled a long breath of relief. Dad listened better to Dessie than to her or Irene. The older woman, her best friend's mother, had a reputation as a healer. Even Dad respected her air of authority.

Dessie pulled a needle from her bag and held it up. Jolene took it to the kitchen and lifted the front lid on the stove. Holding the needle with a pair of pliers from the work drawer, she extended it over the flames a few seconds. Then she took it back to the bedroom.

As she held her dad's leg in place for Dessie to stitch it, Jolene's stomach knotted at the sight of the horrible wound and the reddened area around it. To help block out the sound of Dad's groans, she let her mind envision Riley hunkered down on the low milk stool out in the barn. He had lost none of his affect on her.

As soon as Dessie finished, Jolene got out of the room, fighting to keep her stomach from emptying. In the kitchen, Irene stood at the stove, stirring a pot of potato soup. She appeared on the verge of tears. More accurately, she looked like she had been crying.

Irene looked around at her. "Do you think I should stay home from school tomorrow and look after Dad?"

Jolene shook her head. "You can't miss that big math test you've been studying for all week."

"But you have to teach."

Irene was right. As a rural teacher, Jolene didn't get time off for vacations or sickness. Any days she missed would have to be added to the end of the school year. Dad knew all that and would never hear of her staying home to "babysit" him.

She wiped a hand across her brow, too tired to think. "Let's talk about it after we eat and get the work done."

A scream from outside the house made them both jump. Jolene dashed to the door and jerked it open. At the edge of the yard she saw that Riley had a young boy gripped by the shoulders, marching him toward the house, the kid kicking and yowling in protest. In a move of exasperation, Riley yanked the boy up under his arm and carried him. Twisting and struggling, the boy almost got away, but Riley tightened his hold and kept walking.

Jolene stepped out the kitchen door to meet them.

When Riley set the boy on his feet, she saw his face for the first time. "Why, what's the matter, Kurt?" She gripped the boy's shoulders and stooped to peer into his face.

"I milked one cow and set the bucket aside while I milked the other one," Riley explained when the boy didn't speak. "I heard something and looked around. This young man was scooping milk outa the bucket with his hands, slurping it down."

Jolene stared at Kurt. He was small for an eight-year-old, but still heavy enough to have her straining to hold on to him. She squatted before him. "You're hungry, aren't you, Kurt?"

His head bobbed, his overlong blond hair nearly obscuring his eyes.

"Where are your parents?"

His mouth locked in mutinous silence.

She looked up at Riley in the fading light. "He's tired and hungry."

"I'll finish milking while you feed him."

Jolene didn't have time to watch his departing figure the way she would have liked. She got to her feet, keeping a firm grip on Kurt's hand. "Let's find you something to eat."

She led her former student inside and pressed him into a chair at the table. Then she poured him a glass of milk.

"Here's some corn bread," Irene said as she pulled a pan from the oven. She cut a piece and put it on a saucer. Jolene buttered it and took some bacon from the platter Irene was filling.

The boy shoveled food into his mouth like he hadn't had anything all day. Jolene sat in the chair near the corner of the table where she could be at eye level with him. "Did you come out here this morning instead of going to school?"

Kurt swallowed and gave a silent nod, his eyes not fully meeting hers.

"Why did you do that? Don't you know your parents are worried about you?"

His lip trembled, but he finally spoke. "I hate that school. The kids talk mean and make fun of me because I'm from the country."

Oh, dear. Jolene understood only too well how hurtful children could be to one another. "But you have to go to school. Your mom and dad want you to learn things that will help you as you grow up."

He gulped, and one big tear oozed from the corner of

his eye. "I know. I want to do that. But I can't go to that school. Can't I come back to your school?"

Kurt was not the brightest scholar she had taught in her seven years at the Deer Creek School, but he had never been a problem child and he worked as hard as any of the children. It broke Jolene's heart to see him so unhappy.

Riley came to the door with the full milk pails. He hesitated before entering.

"Come on in," she invited. She got up and took one of the buckets. As she set it on the table, Irene took the other bucket and said, "I'll strain it."

Jolene glanced down at the unhappy child. "Can you also watch Kurt for a few minutes?"

Irene looked at Riley and then back at Jolene. "Sure."

Jolene spoke to Riley in a low voice. "Let's step outside."

Understanding from her manner that she wanted to speak to him away from the boy's hearing, he accompanied her back out the door and stood next to her in silence. Jolene swallowed as Riley's black eyes raked over her bedraggled appearance, self-conscious about her worn and faded dress. Goose bumps covered her arms in the dropping temperature. She rubbed them and spoke fast so they could get back inside. "The Sullivans lost their farm to foreclosure. I don't know where they went."

His expression remained taciturn as he weighed her words. "You mean his parents."

"Yes."

"I'll take Mom home and come back. Then we'll take the kid to town. Leon will know where to find the family."

Leon Gentry was the town marshal and Riley's sister's brother-in-law. Riley's younger sister, Callie, was married to Trace, the marshal's younger brother. Jolene didn't like the idea of riding around with Riley, but he was right. Kurt had to be returned to his parents as soon as possible.

Riley looked past her at the door. "I'll get the buckboard ready. Tell Mom to meet me in five minutes. I'll bring her back in the morning," he added before turning to leave.

Jolene went to her dad's bedroom and found Dessie Blake putting on her coat. They walked quietly out of the room together, and Jolene closed the door behind them.

"Sam's not happy at bein' laid up," Dessie said. "Which is to be expected. But I warned him again of what harm he can do if he goes back to work too soon. Get him to eat when he wakes up. I'll be back in the morning to make sure he stays in that bed, even if I have to tie him in it, while you gals go to school. That leg needs to be watched, the bandage changed twice a day, and more ointment put on it."

Dessie patted Jolene's arm. "Now go ahead and eat with your sister. I'll see myself out."

Jolene knew better than to argue with the woman. She had spent a lot of time in the Blake home while she and Callie Blake were growing up and going to school together. She looked to Dessie as her second mother and obeyed her the same as Callie.

"Thank you for your help," she said simply and gave Dessie a hug.

Riley had returned and stood waiting in the doorway. Jolene wished she could read his thoughts. No, based on his rigid expression, she guessed she didn't.

Riley eyed the boy at the table and remembered how much compassion Jolene had always shown toward children. She was good with kids, born to be a teacher—and a mother. Too bad she didn't have the same forgiving attitude toward adults who made mistakes.

Without speaking, he turned and followed his mother to the buckboard. On the way home he listened while she talked.

"I'm real glad to have you home, Riley," she said after she finished telling him about Sam's injury and had her questions about the boy answered. "The holidays will be nicer havin' you here."

Clementine had supper waiting when they got home. Riley ate quickly and got up. "I'm going back to the Delaneys to help Jolene take the runaway kid to town."

"What kid?" Clem asked.

"Mom can tell you about it." He grabbed his hat from its peg on the wall and left.

Back at the Delaney farm, Jolene came out of the house with the boy as Riley pulled the buckboard to a stop. "Have you eaten?" she asked.

"Yeah," he grunted.

"There's gas in the car. I'll drive." She headed for the 1927 Model T.

Bossy woman. But he followed her and crawled into the passenger seat. Seated between them, the boy couldn't run away.

The temperature had dropped to almost freezing. A stirring of wind made the barren treetops sway in the stark woods each side of the country road. "Feels like it might snow," he commented to break the uneasy silence.

Her eyes didn't leave the road. "I guess it would be pretty to have snow on the ground for Thanksgiving next week, but I don't want the roads piled with it."

He nodded. These country roads got in bad enough shape without snow.

"This poor old car might not make it through a tough winter," she said, peering intently ahead into the beam of the headlights.

If he didn't know her better, Riley would think she was nervous. "It's been a good one."

"If it weren't for Trace helping us, it would have fallen apart long ago."

"He's okay."

He didn't really want to talk to her. He didn't really want to be here. But he needed to be sure the kid got home safely, since he was the one who had found him.

When they got to town, Leon wasn't at the jail.

Riley spoke to Jolene over the boy's head. "You know where Leon lives?"

She nodded. "I hate to bother him this late, but I don't know what else to do." She drove on across town to Leon's house.

Riley followed her to the door with Kurt, but stayed back from the steps. The marshal, his brown hair tousled, answered her knock in his stocking feet. His eyes traveled over her and then back to Riley and the kid. "Is there a problem?"

"Kurt ran away from home and hid in our barn. We want to return him to his mother," Jolene explained.

Leon Gentry eyed the boy. "Mr. Sullivan left to look for work in the city. Mrs. Sullivan and the kids are staying in her sister's garage. You passed the place on your way into town."

"You mean the Garth Sullivan place about a mile out?" Riley asked.

The marshal nodded. "That's the one. Do you need me to go out there with you?"

Riley shook his head. "We'll be fine. Thanks for your help."

"Young man," the marshal addressed the boy in a stern voice. "You shouldn't worry your parents like this. And you've put Miss Delaney to a lot of unnecessary trouble."

Kurt looked down, his toe digging a hole in the dirt with its back and forth motion. He still refused to speak.

They took Kurt back to the car. When they drove up a few minutes later, they found a mother who looked to be near the end of her rope.

Mrs. Sullivan hugged Kurt to her, too distraught to scold him. "Thank you, Miss Delaney. We wuz so worried about him. We looked everywhere. Karen walks home with him after school, and she was terrible upset when he didn't meet her."

A peek inside the garage revealed only a stove in the corner, a sofa, a table and pallets on the floor.

Riley noticed a girl who looked to be twelve or thirteen sitting on the old sofa. She had obviously been crying. Two younger children hovered near the doorway, a boy who looked about five, and a girl younger than two.

"He told me he hates the town school," Jolene said to Mrs. Sullivan.

The woman clamped down on her trembling lip. "I know. But we're close enough to town now that he has to go to school there."

"I'm sorry you're unhappy," Jolene told Kurt. "But you have to go to school. I'll pray for you to be strong and learn to deal with it. Okay?"

Kurt did not answer.

They left, but Riley could tell that Jolene was troubled. "He'll be okay," he said when they got back in the car.

Neither of them talked during the mile drive back to the Delaney farm. Riley got out as soon as she parked the car. "I'll be here early in the morning to do chores. Then I'll bring Mom over in the afternoon to check on

Sam," he said before going to hitch the horses back to the buckboard.

Sunday went well. Riley got up extra early and went to do chores at the Delaney farm, finding it a good excuse to avoid the usual pressure from his parents to attend church with them. That afternoon, as promised, he took his mom over to check on Sam.

Monday morning he took her back again and did Sam Delaney's chores. Then he went home to cut logs with his dad the rest of the day. While Clem fixed supper that evening, he went back to the Delaneys to do evening chores and get his mom. He felt like a rat running in circles.

Irene met him at the door with the milk buckets. "Jolene just got home from school. She's in her room."

Like he needed to know that. "I'll hurry along and be back for Mom soon as I finish the chores. Shouldn't be more than an hour or so."

When he returned from the barn with the milk, another buckboard sat parked in front of the house. He went around to the back door and knocked, not wanting to interrupt visitors.

Jolene opened the door, her expression troubled. "Kurt's mother and her other kids are here. He's disappeared again."

Chapter 2

For He shall give His angels charge over thee, to keep thee in all thy ways. Place Your angels around Kurt, Lord. Please keep him safe, Jolene quoted and prayed silently as she exited the house to meet Riley. She was relieved to have him there. He might not like her, but he wouldn't refuse to help find Kurt.

He frowned. "Did they come straight here looking for him?"

Mrs. Sullivan moved up behind Jolene, the tiny tot in her arms, the five-year-old clinging to her skirt. Karen, Kurt's sister, hovered behind them. "We done looked everywhere around the place and 'tween there and the town school," the mother said. "Then we came to see if he's here again."

"His pillowcase and a blanket and his other pants and shirt are gone," Karen said.

Jolene watched an odd expression flit across Riley's

face, as though something had occurred to him. "What is it?"

He rubbed the side of his head, as if trying to stimulate his brain. "I don't know where Kurt is," he said slowly, "but I think I know where he's been." He turned and stared back toward the woodpile.

"What is it?" Mrs. Sullivan demanded, rushing out the door to grip his arm. Tears ran down her cheeks.

"I laid my sandwich over there." He pointed at a big piece of log. "It disappeared. I thought the dog got it."

As Jolene understood, she began to move. "Let's check the barn. That's where he hid yesterday."

Together she and Riley ran toward the barn. Mrs. Sullivan and the children followed. They all entered the building calling Kurt's name.

Memories haunted Jolene as they looked in all the nooks and crannies where she and the Blakes had romped and hidden from one another as children. When she climbed up into the loft, it hit her especially hard. This was where she and Callie had hidden when they wanted privacy to play their pretend games and share their girlish secrets. She remembered the day she had confessed to her best friend that she found her brother, Riley, attractive. She shut off those thoughts.

Jolene worked her way around the loft, checking everywhere, even in the rafters where the boy could not possibly have gotten. Suddenly, a spot of color in a pile of hay in a corner caught her attention. She reached into the pile and pulled out a pillowcase made of a feed sack.

"Riley. Mrs. Sullivan," she called in excitement.

Riley came scrambling up the ladder.

"You two stay down here. Karen, hold the baby," she heard Mrs. Sullivan say below them. Moments after Riley stepped off the ladder, the woman's head appeared at the top of it.

Jolene held up the case. "This has to be where he spent the day."

"That's it," Mrs. Sullivan cried as she joined them. "I made that for him. He liked the colors in that sack." She reached for it.

Jolene handed it to her and watched the woman pull out a small pair of frayed overalls and an equally worn shirt. She dug in the case for more, but found nothing. She looked around. "There's no blanket here."

Jolene met Riley's pensive look. "Do you think he went someplace else to sleep?"

Riley ran a hand over his chin. "Why did he run away?"

Jolene followed the direction of his thoughts. "He hates the town school. Do you think he went back to my school?"

"I think it's the next place we should look."

Hope rose in Jolene's chest. "I agree."

Mrs. Sullivan hurried back to the ladder. "Kids, get in the buckboard," she shouted as she began to back down the rungs.

"Mine's hitched. Let's take it," Riley said to Jolene as he waited for her to go ahead of him down the ladder.

Within minutes the two buckboards rattled down the road as fast as the drivers could get their horses to go. Worry made Jolene's stomach churn at the same reckless speed. The barren woods each side of them flashed in her peripheral vision as she stared ahead of them in the dusk at the Sullivan wagon.

When they got to the school, Jolene climbed to the ground and caught up to the upset woman at the steps. While she unlocked the door, Riley ran to a window and peered inside. Then he disappeared around the corner of the building.

"This window is wedged open with a stick," he called, his voice rising.

Jolene opened the door and eased inside, Mrs. Sullivan so close behind her she could feel the woman's breath. "I told Karen to keep the little ones in the wagon," she whispered.

"Kurt? Are you here?" Jolene called.

At first there was silence. Then Jolene thought she heard a muffled sound. She moved on inside the dark room, wishing she had a lantern.

"Kurt, are you here?" his mother called, near hysteria. "Answer us. Please?"

Another sound to her right alerted Jolene. It sounded like crying. She moved toward the stove and saw a small, dark form by the wood box.

Mrs. Sullivan rushed forward and sank to the floor. Her arms went around the boy. "Why, Kurt?" she asked, pulling him to her.

When Jolene squatted beside them, she saw that Kurt was wrapped in his blanket and shivering from the cold.

Riley dropped to his haunches next to them and spoke to him. "You spent the day in the Delaney barn, but came over here sometime during the day and wedged the window open. Then you came back here to sleep, thinking it would be warmer than in the barn, didn't you?"

Kurt sobbed and clung to his mother. "I hate that big school," he wailed. "You can whup me, Ma, but don't make me go back. I'll run away again."

Jolene's heart ached for the little guy, but she didn't know what to do. "Kurt, I'm sorry you don't like your new school. But you shouldn't worry your mom like this.

If I could still have you come here, I'd be happy about it. But I can't change things. Neither can your mom."

"Come on, let's go." His mother got awkwardly to her feet and pulled him up with her.

"Here, let me carry him." Riley took Kurt into his arms. Surprisingly, the boy let him. Probably too cold to insist he was too big to be carried.

They left the building, and Riley handed Kurt up onto the wagon seat to Mrs. Sullivan. "Thank you," she said wearily. "We'll try not to bother you again."

Kurt's continued sobs as the buckboard pulled away broke Jolene's heart. She wished there was something she could do.

"Let's go." Riley's hand over hers startled Jolene. And bothered her in another way. She wanted to jerk it away, but didn't want to offend him. So she let him lead her back to his wagon and assist her up into it.

As they rode back to her house in the dark, the silence became oppressive. "I hope he doesn't run away again," she said in an effort to make polite conversation.

She thought Riley would ignore her, but he finally spoke. "It's too bad what's happened to his folks. Being poor affects the young 'uns, and they can't do anything about it. Don't you ever get mad at God for letting so much bad stuff happen? I mean, your dad was well-off before the banks closed and he lost his money. Then the drought caused him to lose his stock."

"Dad had a hard time at first, I admit," she said stiffly, smoothing the skirt of her rumpled dress over her knees. "He would lie awake at night, unable to sleep. Then he would get up and light a lamp and read his Bible."

"But God didn't get his money back for him, did He?"

Jolene glanced over at the harsh line of Riley's jaw,

barely visible in the dark. "No, He didn't. But we've learned to count our blessings."

He snorted. "You call it blessings working your fingers to the bone just to survive?"

"We're more fortunate than many. We own our land. We have food from our garden and orchard. And I have my teaching position at the school."

As she spoke, Jolene regretted more than ever Riley's refusal to become a Christian, their angry parting so long ago. She hated this stiffness and discomfort between them.

"How secure is your teaching job?"

"I suppose as secure as anything these days. I know the school board's not looking to replace me, because they're more likely to decide to close the school. With money so tight, they asked me to take a thirty percent pay cut. But I still have a job."

"In other words, you figure something is better than nothing."

She nodded. "Irene got paid two dollars a month for doing the janitor work at the school before she finished eighth grade and went on to high school in town. Now she's on the new National Youth Administration program and works in the school library. She gets to spend what she makes on clothes and supplies she needs for school."

"I guess it all helps," he allowed.

"What about you?" She wanted to steer the talk away from herself. She could see his shoulders shrug.

"The Works Progress Administration job I was working on got done, so I took a break before signing on for another one. The folks wanted me to come home for the holidays. Their house is falling apart. The roof is in bad shape, and the chinks and cracks around the windows are awful. I'm helping Dad cut lumber to build a new one in the spring. Business has come to a standstill because nobody has any money to buy lumber for anything, so we have time to cut for ourselves."

"I guess you miss Delmer." She referred to his youngest brother.

"Yeah, but he's better off working for the Civilian Conservation Corps. He signed up when I went to work for the WPA two years ago. He was at the Indian Trail Camp close to Salem for a while, but now he's at the Blooming Rose Camp that opened last year. He has food, clothes and medical care. And the allotment the folks get from his pay really helps."

"Your dad still works at the rock crusher, doesn't he?"

"Yeah. He sharpens the crosscut saws the men use."

"I used to love spending time in his shop with Callie and watching him work at his forge."

Riley turned the wagon in at her house and pulled to a stop. His mother came out the door, wearing her coat. "She must have been watching for us." He hopped to the ground and rounded the wagon in time to assist Jolene to the ground. She edged away from him as he boosted his mother up onto the just vacated seat.

"How's Dad?" she asked Dessie Blake.

"I don't like the color of that leg. I'll be back in the morning to check on it. I hope you all will come to Thanksgiving dinner with us Thursday."

Jolene frowned. "I'm not sure Dad should be on his feet."

"How about if I make him some crutches?" Riley said as he climbed up beside his mom.

Jolene was surprised at his offer, but she shouldn't have been. Riley was as generous and helpful toward his neighbors as the rest of his family—except toward her.

"That's a good idea," his mother said. "If you could get them done by Wednesday evening he could use them Thursday."

"I can do that." He slapped the reins against the rumps of the horses.

Jolene watched them drive off before going inside.

"The chigger stopped by," Irene greeted her as she came through the door. Dressed in the overalls she wore to do chores, she lounged upside down. Her feet stuck up over the back of the sofa, her head lolled back over the center cushion. She held a book in her hands.

"Irene, stop calling Juanita that." Juanita Tomlin was their neighbor to the west, and a member of the same church as the Delaney and Blake families. According to Irene, the woman was like a chigger. She wouldn't kill you, but she sure would irritate you.

"She said she stopped to check on Dad," her little sister went on blithely, "but I bet it was you she really wanted to check on."

Jolene removed her coat. "Someday she's going to overhear you call her that, and you'll be terribly embarrassed."

"You mean *you'll* be embarrassed," Irene amended, rolling her head back to look up at her. "You know she's a busybody."

Jolene pressed her lips together. "She has a need to be recognized and appreciated. Like we all do."

Irene raised her palms in surrender. "Okay, okay."

"Is your homework done?" Jolene asked as she hung her coat on the coat tree by the door.

"It's done," Irene assured her. "That's why I was reading this book I checked out of the school library. What's the use of working there if I can't use it?"

Jolene headed to check on her dad. "You could read your Bible," she said over her shoulder.

"Jolene."

She paused and looked back.

Irene's feet came down, and she turned her body upright. She beckoned with a finger and patted the sofa cushion with her other hand. Something in her younger sister's manner drew Jolene back to sit beside her.

"Dad's fine," Irene said. "Or as fine as he can be. He's sleeping. Don't worry."

Jolene tried to interpret her little sister's expression, but couldn't.

Irene swallowed and hesitated a moment. "Sis, I know I haven't said it enough, but I appreciate how you've taken care of me since Mom died—and before that. But I'm a big girl now. You don't have to do everything by yourself anymore. We can't depend on Mrs. Blake to come over every day and take care of Dad, and you can't afford to miss school. I'll stay home tomorrow and Wednesday and look after him, make sure he doesn't get out of bed and try to go back to work. It won't hurt me to miss a couple of days. We'll see how he's doing by next week and decide then what to do."

A burning attacked the back of Jolene's eyes. Irene had always been her baby sister—talented and sweet—and dependent on her. Now she was suddenly a young lady, albeit a tomboyish one, and ready to share the load.

She reached over and pulled Irene into her arms. "I love you. It's been a joy to take care of you. And you're right. By Thursday Dad may be able to go to the Blakes' for Thanksgiving dinner. Dessie invited us."

"She said she was going to." Irene pulled back and looked into Jolene's face. "We probably shouldn't plan on it, though. Dad can't walk, and we can't handle him."

"Riley said he'll make some crutches for him."

The mention of Riley's name hung in the air between them.

"Will you tell me the truth?" Irene asked softly. "I know you cared a lot about him, and something went terribly wrong." She waited.

Jolene considered what to say. Irene deserved honesty. But how much of her heart could she reveal? "Yes, I cared about him," she admitted at last, clenching her fists in her lap. "I cared too much. I knew he wasn't a Christian, and I lo—cared about him, anyhow. He refused my invitations to church. And he got involved in that bootlegging mess. When I tried to talk to him about his relationship with God, he accused me of preaching at him and said he wanted nothing more to do with me. I've stayed away from him since then."

Irene nodded slowly. "You know I love you, don't you?"

Jolene met her sister's eyes. "Of course I do. What kind of question is that?"

Irene drew in a long, fortifying breath. "I hope you love me enough to let me say something to you."

After a long moment Jolene shrugged. "What?"

"You've changed since then," she said in a rush. "You were always strong and loving, always helping others. You still do that, but you're more…rigid," she said at last. "You quote scriptures and work like a slave. But you're more pious and…judgmental."

Irene hugged her again. "Please don't be mad at me. It just hurts me to see you turning sour and angry."

Jolene's thought processes clashed. Had she really become so hard? "I'm sorry," she whispered. "I didn't realize."

Irene pulled back and patted her shoulders. Then she

smiled. "Don't worry. It's not critical. You just get so busy taking care of everybody and telling them how much God loves them that you forget to remember how much He loves you. I suspect you think you're unlovable, and you're not. Someday some man is going to convince you of that."

Jolene scowled. "That's obviously not God's plan for me. I'll stay single and teach school all my life. And I'll be happy," she promised, wanting to put Irene's mind at ease.

Silence followed her declaration.

"I don't think so," Irene said slowly. "But I'm not going to argue with you about it." She yawned. "Let's go to bed."

Half an hour later, Jolene lay staring up into the darkness, unable to go to sleep. She worried about Kurt Sullivan. And she couldn't stop thinking about Irene's words. Along with all that, images of Riley Blake crowded into her head. She wound the quilts tighter around her and huddled under them.

In spite of her resolve to be less "preachy," concern for Riley's spiritual condition nagged at her. The only times she had ever seen him at church were for special programs that involved members of his family. At no time had she ever seen or heard anything from him that reflected more than a surface acquaintance with the Lord and the church.

"Lord, be near Riley. Work in his heart," she prayed before yielding to sleep.

Riley got a pair of buckets and set out for the schoolhouse across the road. The building sat back a couple hundred yards, centered in a two-acre plot lined by oak trees. The water pump was behind it.

During the drought his dad had made a big tank out of lumber and used it, as well as barrels, to haul water from various springs around the area. They had dug a cistern in the backyard, but hadn't gotten it walled up right and could only use the water they caught in it for baths, dishes and the stock. They carried their drinking water from the cistern at the school.

He went to the pump around back of the building and had it about primed when he heard a commotion from the front of the school. He went to the corner of the building and peered around it.

Children poured from the doorway, shouting and waving their hands in the air.

Chapter 3

Older students led the younger children as they spilled pell-mell down the steps. Once in the yard, they turned to stare back at the doorway.

Riley headed toward it. What in the world had happened? Was Jolene hurt?

She burst through the door, a shoe raised in her right hand. One foot was bare.

He backed up.

"It's all right, children," she announced from the top of the three steps. "I killed them."

Killed them?

"Are you all right?" he asked.

She spun around to face Riley, a hand over her chest. "Oh, you startled me."

He backed away, but his eyes locked on the shoe in her hand. "That's a mean-looking weapon you got there. May I ask who you killed?"

She stared at the shoe, and then the hand moved from her chest to cover her mouth. She muffled a snicker.

"It was hornets," a student called from the school yard.

"A whole nest of 'em," another shouted.

Jolene placed the shoe on the step and pushed her foot into it. "This was the first thing I could get my hands on," she explained. She faced the students. "Children, go back inside and continue your lessons. I threw the nest in the stove and killed the two hornets that got out of it. I'll join you in a moment."

Riley's curiosity got the better of him. "Why did you have hornets in the school?"

She grimaced. "Barry Young brought an old hornet nest this morning to show to the class. I hung it on the wall for display. Later a student noticed a hornet crawling out of it. Then there was another. I told the children to get out of the building, and I threw the nest in the stove."

His mouth twitched. "You did, huh?" Hearing her admit she had made a mistake amused him. "Then you killed the loose ones with your shoe."

She shrugged. "I had to. They're dangerous."

In spite of himself, he found the old attraction for her surfacing, and deepening. It took him by surprise every time he saw her. "I'm glad you saved the kids."

She backed toward the door, so he turned to leave. Then he paused and looked back. "Uh, Jolene?"

She stopped in the doorway.

"I have your dad's crutches almost done. I'll bring them by tomorrow."

"Thank you," she said politely and went inside.

Jolene hurried to the front of the room, struggling to get her mind back onto business. She took time to tie her shoe and take several deep breaths. Seeing Riley again so unexpectedly had shaken her, stirred emotions she wanted buried in the past. She went to the chalkboard to write the spelling word list for the third graders.

When she turned to speak to the students, her eyes automatically focused on the empty desk in the second row. Kurt's unhappy face and heartbroken sobs haunted her. She shook off the thoughts and continued the lesson.

Over the remainder of the day Jolene carried out her duties and kept the children occupied. But at every turn she had to fight the images of Kurt's face. By the time she dismissed the children for the day, she could stand it no longer. So he could finish sooner, she helped Donald, the boy who had taken Irene's place as the paid janitor, with his work. Because the position had been such a help to her and Irene, she had insisted the board not cut it when they lowered her salary. She would mark papers tonight at home.

"Would you like a ride home?" she asked Donald as soon as they finished and she locked the front door.

"Thank you, Miss Delaney, but I guess I'll walk. It's good for me." He grinned in a way that said he knew she understood his wish to stop at his girlfriend's house on the way home.

"All right. See you in the morning."

The car coughed and sputtered, but she finally got it started. "I think I have enough gas," she muttered to herself, thinking of the driving she had to do.

She drove the mile to her house, but passed it and drove another mile and pulled in at the garage where the Sullivans were staying. She bowed her head on the steering wheel. "Lord, give me the right words to say to these people. You know my heart, that I only want to help them."

She got out of the car, trying to squelch the hollow

feeling in her stomach. She had no clear plan, but she had to at least talk to Kurt's mother again. She pulled her coat tighter around her as the cold, damp air seeped through her.

She followed the path around the house to the garage and paused at the door. Breathed another silent prayer as her fingers rapped on the door.

It eased open, and Karen's blue eyes stared up at her. Behind the twelve-year-old, Jolene could see Mrs. Sullivan, Kurt and the two small ones huddling around the woodstove.

"Come in, Miss Delaney." Karen moved back.

Jolene stepped inside the makeshift quarters and swallowed against the sympathy that threatened to overwhelm her. Kurt stared at her with such hope. She had thought life was hard these past few years, but it shamed her to see how much harder it had been for this family. Kurt ran to her and clutched her hand.

"Mrs. Sullivan," she said slowly as the woman got to her feet, toddler in arms, and came across the room. Her face bore lines of weariness and sorrow. Jolene forced her lungs to function against the tightness in her chest and squeezed Kurt's hand. "I don't want to intrude on your family affairs," she said, thinking as she spoke. Her tongue took over. "Would you consider letting Kurt stay at the farm with my family and attend school with me the rest of the term?"

Kurt raised his face in a look of surprised pleading.

Already taken by surprise, Mrs. Sullivan stared at Jolene silently. Then she placed a hand on her chest, backed up, collapsed onto the sofa next to Karen and stared up at Jolene. "I don't know what to say, Miss Delaney. That's such a generous offer. But he's my responsibility."

Jolene released Kurt's hand and went over to perch next to the woman, barely able to fit into the small space left on the cushion. Karen got up and moved closer to the stove. Kurt squeezed into the spot she had vacated and snuggled up to Jolene. "Please, Mama," he begged.

Mrs. Sullivan stared at her son, and then looked over at Karen.

"It's all right, Mama," the girl said. "He's not happy here, and he has to go to school. I'll carry in the wood in his place."

"He could still be here weekends," Jolene pointed out.

"I'd carry extra wood then and help with all the work, Mama." Kurt's small face wrinkled, and he clenched his hands. He left Jolene and crawled onto his mother's lap. His arms went up around her neck. "I don't want to leave you, Mama," he sobbed. "But I want to go to school, and I can't go to that one." His tone made it clear which one he meant.

Jolene couldn't say any more. The decision had to be between the mother and child.

The woman peered over Kurt's head, tears in her eyes. "If I let him go, will you make him help you with chores?"

Jolene nodded. "I can find plenty for him to do."

Kurt twisted around to face her, his dark eyes somber. "I'll be good and do whatever you say, Miss Delaney. I'll study hard, too."

Mrs. Sullivan stared up at the ceiling and blinked. Then she drew in a long breath. "Okay." She set Kurt on the floor. "Get your other clothes and put on your coat. Miss Delaney," she said as he ran to follow orders, "I don't know how to properly thank you."

"You just concentrate on your other kids and let me help with this one," Jolene said.

Minutes later she and Kurt got into her car and drove back to the farm. Irene met them at the door. "I was worried about you," she greeted them. "But I see you've brought us a..."

"Boarding student," Jolene finished for her.

Kurt grinned, and his eight-year-old chest puffed out. "Yeah. I'm going back to my old school with Miss Delaney."

Irene looked from one to the other and opened her mouth to say more, but then closed it, her look saying she would save her questions for later. Jolene nodded a silent message that they would talk about it in private.

"How's Dad?"

"Mrs. Blake said he's being cantankerous, wanting to get up and work. But she said it's too soon. We should hog-tie him if necessary to keep him in the house." Irene grinned. "Maybe Kurt can keep him company this evening. Supper's ready."

Wednesday morning Kurt was up and dressed early. He even seemed disappointed when he realized that school would be dismissed early that day for the Thanksgiving holiday and not resume until Monday.

That afternoon Jolene sent Kurt into her dad's bedroom to keep him company and run errands for him while she baked a blackberry cobbler and made a double batch of sugar cookies to take to the Blakes the next day. Irene divided her time between looking after their dad and doing outside chores, having sent Mrs. Blake and Riley home as soon as she got home from school.

Thursday morning Jolene got up early and made a big pot of chicken and dumplings. When Riley drove up at eight, she finished wiping the table from breakfast and went to the door.

"Mom said she'll take a look at Sam's leg when we get

to the house," he said, crutches in hand. "Do you want to ride in the buckboard with me?"

"I think it would be easier to get Dad into the car." She met the gaze he had fastened onto her. When it turned to a lopsided grin, her heart faltered and jumped like marbles on a hard surface, much to her dismay. Where was her common sense? She knew better than to let his charm get to her.

She spun on her heel and went to get her coat.

When he drove up to his parents' house, Riley saw Trace Gentry in the yard with his three little ones, almost four-year-old Lily and the eighteen-month-old twins, Luke and Lane. The tall, dark-haired man had his hands full, carrying one twin and trailing the other, while Lily romped hither and yon.

Funny how a man changed, turned all domestic, when he got roped in by a woman. Babies. Church all the time. Woman stuff.

There had been a time when his own yearnings had drifted that way. But the gal in his mind wanted him to fall in line with her ideas and started preaching at him about how important God ought to be to him and was always trying to drag him to church. His folks called themselves Christians and attended church all the time, but he had no use for a God who had let his fifteen-year-old brother die in a senseless accident when Riley was eight. Over the years he and his younger brother, Delmer, had skipped services a lot and done some unlawful things. He figured God had no use for a guy like him, with his history of mistakes and mischief.

The Delaney car pulled in just then. He hopped off the buckboard and went back to meet them and help Sam into the house. A large, muscular man, Sam outweighed him by at least thirty pounds. He and Jolene steadied him on either side. Once they got him inside and settled into a chair, they sort of tiptoed around one another. She had the Sullivan kid and her sister with her. They each carried containers of food.

Delicious smells met them at the door. His sisters, Callie and Clem, and his mom had been busy for hours preparing a big spread. Though the house was smaller than Trace and the Delaney clan were used to, they didn't seem to be bothered by it.

Before leaving that morning, Riley and his dad had brought in a couple of sawhorses and laid planks across them to form a table along one wall of the kitchen. A green-checked tablecloth covered it.

"We can eat soon as Clem gets the drinks poured," his mother called from the kitchen stove.

Riley glanced through the doorway at Clem, working alongside the other women, and was thankful for the way she had settled down after being rather wild as a girl. She had a sweetheart, but Joe had enlisted in the army after failing to find a job when he quit high school. They planned to marry after he finished his military hitch. Riley went to the front door and stuck his head out. "Trace, you better get those kids in here if you're gonna eat with us."

By the time everyone got inside, the house was packed tight, but no one minded.

His dad sat at the head of the table and bowed his head. So did everyone else, including Riley, because it was the polite thing to do. "Lord, we thank You for all this fine food, and for having the family with us," Arlie prayed. "Please be with Delmer and the older girls. Amen."

"Riley killed the turkey," Clem said when the prayer ended.

"I want to hunt a turkey," Kurt piped up.

"Maybe sometime." Jolene placed a slice of meat on his plate.

The kid turned adoring eyes on her. "I can still say this week's memory verse, Miss Delaney. 'For all have sinned, and come short of the glory of God.' Romans three, twenty-three," he quoted proudly.

Good grief. She was brainwashing little kids in school, just like Miss Cross had done before her. Riley guessed it wouldn't hurt them, but he wasn't convinced it would help, either. It hadn't helped him.

Jolene praised the boy, and the conversation moved on. The ebb and flow as dishes were passed back and forth kept Riley from having to participate very much. He mostly responded to questions.

"Now, just because you're full and drowsy doesn't mean you get to lie down and go to sleep," Callie said when they finished dessert. She focused on Sam Delaney. "Do you feel like cracking and hulling some walnuts for our Christmas baking? Mom, Jolene and I were comparing notes, and our supplies are getting low."

"Bring 'em on," Sam said with a grin.

"It may be a holiday, but I have chores to do." Arlie pushed his chair back.

"I'll help you," Trace said, following him to the door.

Riley started to get up and go with them, but Callie forestalled him. "We need someone to gather more walnuts. Jolene said she and Kurt will go to the creek and pick up some, but they could use help. I have to stay with my babies and help Mom, Clem and Irene clean up. Will you go?"

Riley glared across the table at his sister, then looked at Jolene, suspecting they had been set up. He couldn't think of a way out of it that wouldn't be rude. He swallowed a lump of frustration and got to his feet. "I'll go to the barn and get some gunnysacks."

As Riley went out the door, Jolene scowled at her best friend who, with huge black eyes and black hair, was still pretty after five years of marriage. "You're in trouble, Callie Gentry."

Callie grinned and adopted an air of innocence. Jolene couldn't help but notice that Mrs. Blake and Clem both seemed suddenly extra busy. Admitting defeat, she drew a breath of exasperation. "All right, I'll go get your walnuts. But that's all."

Callie removed the tablecloth from the just cleared makeshift table. "I don't expect anything else. I just want you to relax and enjoy the rest of the afternoon. We don't need your help with the dishes," she added, forestalling any offer to help. "There's not enough room for too many cooks in the kitchen." Her grin was cheeky.

A tiny twin toddled into the kitchen, claiming her attention. While Callie scooped up her child, Jolene went to get her coat. Once she had it on, she went to the door and looked outside for Kurt. He sat on the cold ground, petting the family dog, a black mutt. She went out to join him.

Riley came around the corner of the house holding up a handful of burlap bags. "I got enough for all three of us. Are you two ready to go?"

Resigned, Jolene set out toward the road. Leaves littered the yard and tumbled about in the wind that blew from the north. It carried what felt like a change of weather on the way. She looked out over the landscape and judged that their first snow could commence at any time.

"Let's go." She held out a hand to Kurt.

"Where are the walnuts?" the boy asked, ignoring her hand.

"Down below that field along the creek bank." She pointed across the road.

He scampered off ahead of her, foiling her intention to keep him between herself and Riley. She set out to catch him.

"Hey, what's the hurry?" Riley demanded, catching up to her. "Are you running away from me?"

She slowed down and looked sideways at him. "What if I am? You don't have to tag along with me just because your sister obligated you. If I didn't like her so much, I'd strangle her."

He grinned, seemingly unfazed by her snippy tone. "You noticed that, did you?"

"How could I miss it?"

"She means well." He seemed unconcerned.

"Maybe you should set her straight, tell her you don't want anything to do with me."

"Maybe you should tell her you don't want anything to do with me," he countered.

Jolene quickened her pace and caught up with Kurt, who was skipping along, swinging his sack around him every which way.

Oddly nervous, Jolene recognized the foolishness of being alone with Riley again. Would she never learn to steer clear of him, no matter how she had to do it?

"You don't have to run from me. I won't bite you."

His voice at her side startled her. "Don't sneak up on me like that," she snapped, and then realized how surly she sounded. "Sorry."

"Why don't we forget about everything but gathering

walnuts for the next hour or so," he suggested, keeping pace beside her.

She gazed over at the big pond to their right. He had a point. Kurt had turned around to frown in puzzlement at them. No sense arguing in front of her young charge.

"See that pond?" she asked the boy. "That's where we used to swim in the summer when I visited here."

He nodded. "Wish I could do that."

"Maybe you can," Riley said. "I'll bring you down here if you come out next summer."

Kurt's face brightened. "Can I bring Karen?"

Riley darted Jolene a questioning look.

"That's his older sister," she whispered.

"Sure, you can bring her. Bring your whole family if you want."

They walked over the rise and down the hill. Walnut trees lined the bank of the dry creek. The green-hulled nuts littered the ground and lay between the rocks in the creek bed.

"I'll go down there," Kurt announced, trotting on down the hill. He hopped over the shallow bank, dragging his sack behind him, and began to drop nuts into it.

"I'll start under this tree. You can take that one," Jolene said to Riley, pointing at the one a little farther up the bank.

"Yes, ma'am." His tone was mocking.

She put her hand over her mouth. "I'm sorry. I'm used to telling students what to do."

"I'll let you get away with it this time." He turned and went to work.

They each concentrated on filling their sacks. After a while Jolene stood upright, her back stiff from bending over so much. As she stretched her muscles, a light fall of snow bathed her face. She stuck out her tongue.

"Your face is red." Riley approached, towing his sack behind him.

She looked straight into his eyes, and her breath caught in her throat. Warmth flowed into her freezing cheeks. Near panic gripped her. She yanked her eyes away. She should never have come out here with him.

"I'm glad we don't have school tomorrow," she said breathlessly, needing to make impersonal conversation. "Irene loves being out in the snow."

"And you do, too."

She nodded. "Irene will probably go to the church to play the piano. She most always goes on Saturday, but this will give her an extra opportunity to practice."

"She plays for church?" He twisted the top of his sack.

Jolene beamed with pride. "She started playing for church when she was twelve. She's very talented, and local groups often ask her to play for them."

"Why does she have to practice at church? Don't you have a piano at home?"

Jolene's face dimmed. "No. I wish we did. But we haven't been able to afford one."

His expression turned thoughtful. "When I had dinner at Callie and Trace's house one night last week, Trace mentioned that the town school is getting a new piano."

"His mother's on the school board, so his information should be accurate." Suddenly she realized what he was thinking. "What do you think they plan to do with the old one?"

"I don't know, but I'll ask Trace if you want. Maybe they would sell it at a price you can afford."

She couldn't afford any price, but she didn't admit

that to him. She bit her lower lip. "It can't hurt to find out, I suppose."

As the words left her mouth, she was struck by the total silence around them. She looked over at the empty creek bed, and panic hit her with the force of a gunshot.

"Where's Kurt?"

Chapter 4

"Kurt!" Jolene shouted toward the creek as her feet carried her in that direction. Her stomach rolled. Why had she taken responsibility for an eight-year-old boy who had already run away twice? She should have her head examined.

With Riley at her side, they ran down the small embankment and headed up the creek line. They found no sign of Kurt.

Lord, send Your heavenly guardians to protect Kurt. Help us find him. Please.

Jolene slipped on the rocks that were wet from the sprinkling of snow. Riley's hand that grasped her arm to steady her added to her panic. How could he affect her at such a time? She blinked and brushed clinging snowflakes from her lashes. When she opened them, she squinted ahead and began to run.

A hundred yards or so up the creek bed she dropped to

her knees beside a lump of burlap. She picked up Kurt's sack and peered inside. "He left his walnuts. Why?"

Riley gazed around, pausing to note a squirrel scampering up a tree along the bank, and then looked down at the rocks. "There's a footprint." He pointed at a larger rock where enough snow had accumulated to hold an impression.

Jolene noted the direction it pointed. "He left the creek bed there."

Together they climbed the bank and headed back up the long, inclined hill, checking for more footprints. "Here's one." Riley altered his route slightly.

Being out here, following Riley, caused memories to spiral through Jolene's mind. She and Riley had roamed this valley and ridden… "Riley," she shouted as she remembered the horses. "I bet he spotted Daisy and Baldy and followed them."

He grabbed her hand when she stepped on one of the decaying hedge apples that littered the ground. Her foot slipped and turned her ankle, but his support saved her from a fall. He tugged her after him up the hill. "They were probably headed to the barn."

This was a second, smaller barn that was nothing more than a simple shelter with a couple of stalls. Arlie and the boys stored extra hay there, and the horses went in and out of the doorless opening at will.

Jolene puffed for breath as they topped the long hill and neared the small building.

"Kurt," she called again.

At the door, Riley stopped and let her go ahead of him. And there sat Kurt, in the corner with a bottle in his hand, studying it. The horses stood munching hay from the stalls.

"Why did you take off like that without telling us?"

She squatted next to Kurt, not sure whether to hug him or paddle him. She did the first.

"What's this?" he asked, holding up the bottle.

Jolene froze as seconds ticked by, realizing what it represented. Riley's presence behind them held her motionless.

"It's a liquor bottle," Riley said, a rough edge to his voice. "Some boys used to sneak into this place back when it was illegal for the stuff in those bottles to be around. You should never do such a thing."

Like you and Delmer did.

Kurt held the bottle up with his fingertips. "That was bad, wasn't it?"

Jolene couldn't keep herself from peering around at Riley's face. It was so solemn.

"Yes, it was. Those boys are sorry they did it," he added quickly as if he had to force out the words. "They stopped doing it, but not everyone forgave them."

Remorse struck Jolene's heart. She turned back to face Kurt, unable to look at Riley any longer.

"Give me the bottle." Riley stretched out a hand. "I'll throw it away."

Lord, forgive me. He may not have become a Christian, but he got out of a bad situation. Thank You for that.

As Riley took the bottle and walked away with it, Jolene got to her feet. "The horses are fine, Kurt. But you should not have taken off alone. Let's go back and get our walnuts."

Jolene took his hand and led him out of the building, careful to avoid looking at Riley when they caught up to him. Why did her reaction to Riley's mistake five years ago seem so wrong now? No, she could not have married him. But she could have been more charitable. *For charity shall cover the multitude of sins.*

When Kurt pulled his hand free, she did not object, and watched the boy trot ahead of them. Then it struck her how alone it left her and Riley. Near panic gripped her. Why did he still unnerve her? How could he attract her, yet repel her? She licked her dry lips.

"I'm glad you stopped selling moonshine for the Lonigans," she said in a shallow voice. "I'm sure God was pleased, too."

"It was a mistake. The folks needed money, and I let Troy talk me into it."

The Lonigans had been arrested and spent time in jail. All the money they had made from their moonshine sales was used up paying fines. Jolene couldn't feel sorry for them, but she prayed that their two younger sisters, Zona and Zada, would never be drawn into the shifty activities of their dad and brothers.

Riley could see Jolene's discomfort. Feel it. On one hand he felt bad about it. On the other, he didn't care if she felt a little of the unworthiness she had made him feel years ago. He'd loved her, and had hoped she loved him. But all she had been interested in was whether he lived his life according to her standards.

Turmoil whirled through him. He fought to control it. "You haven't forgotten the past any more than I have."

She brought her eyes around to his, and paused to inhale deeply. She shoved her hands into the pockets of her gray coat. "Are you going to hate me forever?"

Automatically, a hand clamped onto her arm and pulled her to a halt. "I don't hate you. Never did." He fell into the pool of her soft brown eyes, swallowing against the pain of loss. If only he had been stronger, done things differently. But he hadn't.

"I believe you did." Her voice held a sorrow that made

his heart skip. "You're a good man, Riley. You work hard and do all you can to take care of your parents. You always did. I never faulted you for that. It's why I…wanted to be your friend," she finished after a brief falter.

He studied her mouth, her eyes. "We were friends, weren't we?"

She drew herself more erect and met his look eye to eye. "I thought we were. But I guess it wasn't strong enough to weather our differences. I…"

"Hey, are you guys coming?"

Kurt's yell snapped them back to attention, a relief to Jolene. "We're coming," she called back to him.

When they got back to the house, Jolene's dad immediately reached for his coat he had draped across the back of his chair. A dishpan of walnut hulls sat beside him on the floor.

"Chores are waiting." Sam pushed himself out of the chair and tucked the crutches under his arms. It was slight, but Riley detected a grimace of pain. He hoped Sam was all right.

"Here, Sam, let me help you." He reached for the man's shoulder.

"I'm okay." Sam took a deep breath and leaned forward on the crutches, resisting any assistance. When he shifted his injured leg, his jaw tightened, but he hobbled forward. He started to move again, but stopped and took another deep breath.

Riley moved close to him and pulled an arm over his shoulder, determined to help the man, whether he wanted it or not. As he did so, he read a look on Jolene's face that looked like appreciation.

"Kurt. Irene. Come on," she called over her shoulder.

Leaning on Riley, Sam slowly made his way out the door. It took some careful maneuvering to get down the two steps, but they made it. "I think you should see a doctor," Riley said as he helped Sam into the car.

"No, I'll be fine," the man insisted stubbornly. "I'm just stiff from sitting so much today. I need to move around more."

Riley had no choice but to close the car door and watch Jolene, her sister and the Sullivan kid climb in and drive away.

"Sit there until we get around the car to help you out," Jolene ordered her dad when they got home. She had noticed the way he tried to hide his pain, and how much of his weight Riley had supported getting him to the car.

"Are you this bossy with your students?" he barked.

"Yes, she is," Irene said from the backseat. "And they obey."

He shook his head and gave a snort, but he waited. Jolene got on one side of him, Irene on the other, and helped him out of the car. They didn't even bother with the crutches at that point, since Sam seemed too tired to deal with them.

When they got him inside, they settled him on the sofa.

"I want to take a look at that leg," Jolene said in a no-nonsense tone. Sam didn't even put up a fight. She peeled back the bandages and nearly gasped aloud at the sight of the discolored, puffy wound. "Irene, do we have any warm water in the stove reservoir?" she called over her shoulder.

"It's not warm, but it's not real cold," Irene called back moments later.

"Put a teaspoon of salt in about a pint of it and bring it to me."

"Be right there."

Sam laid his head back against the sofa and stared up

at the ceiling, his paleness making Jolene's insides twist with worry. He didn't object when she set a kitchen chair in front of him and lifted his foot onto it. She took the pan of water Irene handed her and bathed the wound, praying as she worked, and hoping the salt water would aid healing as well as cleanse it.

"It looks kind of nasty," Irene commented. "Do you want that quart jar of herb water Mrs. Blake left yesterday?"

"Yes." Bless Riley's mother.

By the time they placed a cloth soaked in the herb water on the leg and rebandaged it, and then got their dad into bed, Jolene and Irene were so tired they had forgotten about Kurt. The sight of his small form slumped in an overstuffed chair, watching them in silence, drew Jolene up short.

She dropped down to his level. "Oh, Kurt, you've been so quiet and good. Thank you. Are you hungry?"

A glance at the clock told her it was past suppertime. But she didn't feel hungry.

"No, Miss Delaney. I ate a lot today." A hand rubbed his stomach.

She knew of nothing more they could do at that moment, so she poured her nervousness into cleaning the kitchen she had left so hurriedly that morning.

The next morning Irene finished her chores and got out her bicycle. "I won't stay too long," she promised as she swung her foot over the center and perched on the seat.

Jolene smiled. If she didn't get to having too much fun. Of course, the frigid cold might make it too difficult for Irene to play the piano for very long in the unheated church.

As Jolene turned to go back inside the house, she spotted a small figure coming on foot around the curve at the corner of the field. She watched until the figure got close enough for her to be sure she recognized the little girl. She hurried inside. "Kurt, your sister is coming."

Kurt ran to the door and peered out, impatience written in his twitching body. He and his sister were close. Jolene liked that. They would draw strength from one another.

"I came to walk Kurt home," Karen announced when she climbed the steps and stopped on the top one. Her cheeks and nose were red beneath a worn scarf.

"Come in," Jolene invited from the doorway. "It's freezing out there."

"Just until Kurt's ready to go," she said politely. "Mama needs us to carry in wood. Uncle Carl cut up a big pile this week."

Jolene could see that the girl was shivering. "Stand in here by the fire and get warm. I'll drive you home as soon as I take care of my dad."

She left the two children and went to change the bandages on his leg. It didn't look as puffy, but the color still bothered her. Infection was setting in. "You stay in that bed," she ordered when she finished and her dad moved as if to get up. "Don't put any weight on that leg."

"I'm tired of this bed," he grumped. "And there's work I need to be doing."

"Irene milked and split enough wood for today." She pressed his chest to keep him in place.

He rubbed a hand over his unshaven chin. "Why did this have to happen?"

"I don't know, Dad. But it did, and you need to be careful until it heals. We'll be fine."

But how? *Help us, Lord, please. Heal Dad's leg. And take care of the Sullivan family.*

As she returned to the living room, she paused at the door, the conversation between the two children holding her motionless. Kurt and Karen sat side by side on the sofa, with Karen assuming a too-grown-up pose that reminded Jolene of herself with Irene during the time of their mother's illness and death. She felt an affinity to the girl.

"I wish you could come back to Deer Creek School with me," Kurt said.

A look of longing crossed Karen's thin face. "I wish I could, too. But even if Miss Delaney could take us both, I couldn't leave Mama. She needs help with the little ones."

The vision of her dad's stoic efforts to hide his pain crossed Jolene's mind, triggering an idea. Making another instant decision, she took her coat from the closet where she had put it only minutes earlier. "I'll go start the car. You two wait and come out when it's had time for the motor to warm up," she said, hoping it would start in the cold.

Thank You, Lord, she breathed silently when the motor sputtered to life after only three tries. She sat shivering while it idled, not wanting to have it die on her if she took off too soon. After a couple minutes she honked the horn. The kids came out and got into the backseat. "Put that blanket over your legs," she said over her shoulder, thankful that they kept one back there.

When they arrived at the garage the Sullivans called home, Jolene got out and went inside with the children. Mrs. Sullivan turned from the stove, surprise filling her face. "Hello, Miss Delaney. Thank you for bringing the kids home, but you didn't have to do that."

Now that she was here, Jolene struggled with how to phrase her proposal to the woman. "Mrs. Sullivan, I…"

The woman flashed a palm in the air. "My name is Georgia."

Jolene smiled, glad she seemed more at ease with her. She wished she could send the children away so she could speak in private, but there was no place to send them. "Georgia, I need your help."

The woman frowned and pushed back a strand of her straggly brown hair. "Of course. What in the world can I do for you?"

Jolene took a deep breath. "You can go home with me. My dad had an accident with the ax, and his leg looks like it's getting infected. I need you to come stay with us and take care of him so my sister and I can go to school and not worry about him."

Furrows formed across her forehead. "You mean for a few days, right?"

"I mean until the end of the school year. Karen could go to school with me and Kurt."

Georgia gasped and covered her mouth with a hand. "You can't be serious."

Jolene edged a few steps closer and looked her in the eye. "I'm dead serious."

Her eyes darted back and forth. Kurt and Karen stood frozen behind them, waiting for their mother to speak. She seemed to take forever to think about it. "I could help with the housework and cooking," she said at last as if talking only to herself.

"And we could help with chores," Karen blurted, hope ringing in her voice.

Georgia turned and looked at her older children. Then she turned back to face Jolene. "Are you sure?"

Jolene nodded. "I'm sure. We can help one another."

Georgia's face scrunched up, and tears flooded her eyes. "When do you want us to come?"

"Right now."

The squeals that erupted from Kurt and Karen woke the two younger children who had been asleep on the sofa. They hugged their mother around the waist, one on each side, before running to grab their younger siblings.

It only took a half hour to gather their meager possessions and pile everything and everybody in the car. As Jolene prayed she had done the right thing, she felt a sense of peace. What she had told Georgia was true. They could help one another.

"I only have one extra bedroom," she explained as the car bounced along the rutted road.

"That's okay," her passenger said. "We've been getting along in one. Anything you got is bound to be better."

"Irene can help us set up another bed with the old mattress that's stored in the barn."

"That's not necessary," Georgia said. "The older kids can sleep on the floor, and the little ones with me."

"The boys can have the second bed, and the girls sleep with you," Jolene amended.

"Thank you," she whispered and went silent to hold back tears.

When they got to the house, Jolene introduced Georgia to her dad, who was polite enough, but she could tell he didn't like the idea of having a nurse. Then she showed the family to the room that she had given Kurt. While they got settled, she went to the kitchen to start a fire in the cookstove. As soon as she had it going, she took a pan of potatoes to the living room and sat down to peel them.

Georgia Sullivan appeared in the door from the hallway. At the same time, the front door opened and Irene burst through the opening. "You better take your earplugs to church Sunday. The chigger…"

Chapter 5

Jolene rolled her eyes in Georgia's direction and pursed her lips in a "quiet" signal.

"Oh, hi," Irene greeted Georgia without missing a beat. "I didn't know anybody was here, but it's nice to see you."

Jolene smiled at her little sister's princess charming act and said, "Georgia is going to stay with us and help take care of Dad. She's from Newburg, but her husband, Ovie, was a couple years ahead of me in school."

Irene shut the door and looked up, her face beaming. "That's great."

"Your dad's leg doesn't look good," Georgia said. "I should change the bandage again."

Kurt bounced into the room, Karen and the younger ones following behind him. "Karen is going to go back to school with me."

"And help with chores," Karen added.

Irene went to the towheaded five-year-old and squatted before him. "Will you start school soon?"

He brightened. "Next year."

"And what's your name?"

"Nathan." He dipped his head in a bashful manner.

Irene turned her attention to the baby. "And who is this?"

"She's Nola."

Irene reached for the dark-haired little one. "Will you let me hold you?"

The baby eyed her for a moment, and then walked into her open arms.

"Wow, she never does that," Karen exclaimed. "You must be special."

Irene darted a look at Jolene to ask if she was forgiven for the near slip of moments ago.

Jolene smothered a smile with her hand. "She'll make a good mother someday," she said to Karen. *But not for a while.* She hated the thought of her sister growing up and leaving.

"What can we do?" Karen asked, including Kurt with herself.

Irene got to her feet, still holding the baby, and looked toward the kitchen. "I bet we need some butter churned," she said to Karen. "You could do that. And Kurt could grind some coffee."

Sneaky brat. But smart. Irene didn't like to sit in one place long enough to churn butter. They usually took turns at the tedious task. Grinding coffee wasn't as distasteful to her, but it did sound like a good job for Kurt.

"Soon as I get some water I'll take those two with me." Georgia went to the stove while Irene and Jolene set out the dash churn and small square grinder.

Later, while everyone worked, Irene sidled past Jolene

at the kitchen table and whispered in her ear, "The chigger said she's singing special music in church Sunday."

Jolene pounded the bread dough she was kneading. "Maybe it won't be too bad."

Irene snickered. "Yes, it will. She caterwauls, and you know it."

Jolene swatted at her backside as she sauntered away. Having a saucy little sister could be exasperating, but it kept her very much alive.

Riley found the snow that fell over the weekend to be both a hindrance and a help. It made for slow slogging about in the woods. But it sure made it easier to skid the logs they cut.

By Monday morning there had been enough vehicle and foot traffic on the roads to form a packed pair of tracks in them, which meant school would be in session. While they worked at the mill, he kept a watchful eye aimed across the road as the student janitor, then Jolene and then the students arrived. He continued to steal glances when they came out for recess, or when one of the older boys came out to get an armload of wood.

The buzz of the saw ripping boards drowned out any other sounds, but he knew what went on each day over there. If anything unusual happened, he would be aware. Late that afternoon something did happen.

At three-thirty horses, wagons and cars began to arrive to pick up children so they wouldn't have to walk home in the bitter cold and the snowdrifts. After the children filed out of the school and the student janitor left, the only vehicle still parked in the school yard was Jolene's.

At about four-thirty she and two young children came out and got into her car. It took several tries before the motor caught, but she finally put the car in motion. At the edge of the road, she turned the wheels to the right and inched forward. But the afternoon sun had melted the snow enough to make it slick, and the wheels slid in the snow.

Riley's heart wrenched when he saw Jolene attempt to gain control of the car—and fail. As it slid into the ditch, he tossed the board he held onto a pile and shut down the equipment. He turned to tell his dad where he was going, but saw him headed to the house with an armload of wood, already beyond hearing range.

Riley struck out across the field. By the time he reached the road, Jolene and the two kids had piled out of the car and were attempting to push it. Silly woman. He knew she was strong, but did she honestly think she could push a car out of a ditch? "Don't wear yourself out for nothing," he called as he came up behind them. He ignored her put-out expression. "Wait, and I'll bring the horses to pull you out. Get back in the car and out of the wind."

He turned and headed for the barn, taking their obedience for granted, whether Miss High-and-Mighty liked taking orders or not. Yet he felt himself softening toward her. How many teachers took needy students under their wing the way she did?

He hurried, knowing she and the kids had to be freezing. He harnessed the horses and led them to the car, ignoring her when she got out and stood behind him, a kid at either side.

"You'll need to get in and steer," he said when he had the singletree attached to the back bumper.

"You two stay out here," Jolene instructed the children. Then she got behind the wheel and held it steady as he slapped the reins against the horses. They moved a bit and stopped. He gave them another slap, and they strained forward. Slowly the car moved. When he had pulled it backward on to the road, he stopped the team and unhooked them.

Jolene got out and came back to him, wearing a pretty smile that warmed him. He gave her a sideways glance. "You okay now?"

Her eyes glowed. "Yes, thank you, Riley. That was nice of you."

"Yeah. I'm a real nice guy," he muttered, "in a pinch." And then he got out of there.

Jolene's day brightened considerably when she got home and learned from Georgia that her dad's leg had improved slightly.

Thank You, Lord, she breathed silently as she hung up her coat. "Do you think he can get out of bed now?"

Georgia nodded, looking less tired than the night before. "I'll have supper on the table soon. He can use his crutches and come to the table."

"I'll tell him." Jolene went to visit him, her steps lighter, the worry she had forced to the back of her mind all day also lighter.

She found Sam sitting on the side of the bed, reading his Bible. He looked up and raked a hand through his white hair. "Glad you're home. That jailer threatened to tie me down." The words were grumpy, but the gleam in his eyes countered them.

Jolene grinned. "You seem in pretty good spirits for a prisoner."

He chuckled and then turned serious. "Being laid up is a nuisance, but I understand about being careful. At least it's given me some time to read the word of God. I'm afraid I haven't done as much of that lately as I should."

Hands on her hips, she smiled. "See. Good can come from bad. Do you feel like coming to the table tonight?"

His eyes brightened. "You bet."

Irene entered the room, his crutches in her hand. "Let's go, then."

That night Jolene thanked God for what seemed like the beginning of better days. Then she prayed for Riley Blake, who occupied her thoughts way too much. He was a good man, a hard worker and his reputation had been clean since he was shot by a gangster who mistook him for Callie. But his refusal to surrender control of his life to God troubled her without ceasing.

The next day went without mishaps. But while driving home Jolene heard a sound that made her groan. Near the top of the hill, only yards from the house, the motor coughed and the car jerked. Sensing trouble, she quickly steered to the edge of the road. Her eyes burned as she blinked back tears, determined that the children not see her cry.

"What's the matter with it, Miss Delaney?" Karen's small voice asked from the backseat.

"It's old and tired, I guess." *Like I feel right now. Lord, what else can go wrong? What are You trying to tell me?*

Fearing an answer, she opened the door. "Let's go to the house and get warm." She waited for the two to join her on the road. They trudged to the top of the hill and into the yard where Irene was parking her bike at the end of the porch. She turned and came to meet them. "What's wrong?"

Jolene explained about the car. "If you'll hook up the horses, we can pull it on up here. I'll have to wait for payday to get Dave Freeman to come out and look at it. Don't tell Dad, or he'll be out here no matter what."

Irene waved a palm. "Dad's not a real good mechanic,

anyhow. Dave would let you pay him after you get your check next week, but I know how set you and Dad are on not owing anybody."

"You two go on inside," Jolene instructed the children. "Help your mom with supper. And don't mention the car to Dad. Okay?" She gave them both a pointed look.

"Okay," they echoed in unison.

It took almost an hour, but she and Irene, using the horses, got the car into the driveway. "I guess you'll have to get to school the way I do now," Irene said with a cheeky grin.

"I'll tell Georgia to keep Dad away from the windows so he won't notice when I leave the car to ride my bicycle in the morning," she said, too weary to respond to Irene's teasing.

"I'll hitch the buckboard in the morning so Georgia can drive the kids to school," Irene said, planning ahead. "They don't need to be there as early as you, and there's no way you can take them with you on the bike."

"I noticed that Jolene rode her bicycle to school this morning instead of driving the car," Riley commented to his brother-in-law as they tramped through the woods.

Since Trace Gentry's auto business had felt the economic squeeze of the past few years, he had worked out a mutually beneficial arrangement with his brother, the town marshal. On slow days like this one, Leon hung out at the dealership and left a note on the jailhouse door explaining where he was. In turn, Trace shared whatever wild game he was able to bring home, which helped both their food budgets and gave them a break from routine. Riley felt that he also benefited, since he got to spend time with Trace. They had become close friends, and he had missed the guy these past two years while he was away working on WPA jobs.

"Did you find out why she's doing that in this freezing cold?"

Riley glanced over at the look of concern on Trace's face. "Yeah. Her car quit her just before she got home last night. She and her sister pulled it home with the horses. I pulled her out of the ditch in front of the school the day before that."

"Sounds like she's having a rough patch."

"Kurt said he heard her tell her sister she can't get the car fixed until she gets her paycheck." He felt a little guilty, yet glad, at having gone to the school on the pretext of getting water while they were having recess and catching Kurt at the pump to question him.

"I have a little time if you want to take a look at it," Trace said. "Why don't you take your share of these rabbits to your mom while I take mine to the truck. Then we'll go get my toolbox and check it."

Five minutes later, they were on their way. Riley waited in the truck while Trace went into his house to leave the rabbits and get his tools. When he came out, he wore a satisfied look. "Don't tell me you've been kissing your wife," Riley growled as Trace got behind the wheel.

His brother-in-law grinned over at him. "Your sister is sweet. I can't resist her."

Riley snorted. "You're hopeless."

"I'm in love," the man corrected. "Marriage is great. You don't know what you're missing."

"Don't care to know."

Trace started the truck and took off. "Don't you plan to marry someday?"

"I doubt it." He didn't need the headaches.

"What about Jolene? Didn't you used to be sweet on her?"

Riley went tense. He didn't want to talk about Jolene. But Trace was his friend, and the man loved his sister. He whooshed in a deep breath of air. "I reckon so. But that's history. She has no use for the likes of me."

"What do you mean, *the likes of you?*"

"I'm a loner, and I don't go around quoting Bible verses."

Trace took his time before speaking again. "Don't you feel a need for God in your life?"

Riley turned his head and looked out the window. "Don't need anybody but my family—and friends."

"But don't you need help now and then?"

"I help myself." The only person he trusted enough to lean on.

"You should rethink that. God is the best ally you could ever want."

Riley looked over at him now. "You take up preaching when I wasn't looking?"

"Didn't mean to preach. Sorry."

"We'll need a car key." Riley figured it was time for a change of subject.

"You're right. Jolene probably has hers with her. We'll have to ask Sam for his."

They pulled in at the Delaney farm and traipsed to the door. "May we see Sam a minute?" Trace asked when Georgia Sullivan answered his knock.

Jolene had brought the Sullivan boy to Thanksgiving dinner. Then Riley had seen her hauling the kid and his sister to school. Now here was the mother. As he thought about it, Riley could see the benefit of having someone here to help take care of Sam. He knew the man's leg was hurting him bad when he left after Thanksgiving dinner.

"He's sittin' up. Come on in." Georgia opened the door wider and stepped back.

"We don't want to track snow inside the house," Trace said. "Will you ask him if we can have a key to his car? We want to see if we can figure out what's wrong with it."

"What in the world are you talking about in there?" Sam called from the next room, obviously having overheard them.

"Jolene had car trouble," Trace called back.

"First I heard of it," Sam retorted. "If that girl don't beat all. Thinks she has to take care of everything herself. Does she know you're here?"

"No, sir. Riley saw her arrive at school on her bicycle. He asked…" He paused and gave Georgia an apologetic look. "He found out from Kurt that she wasn't driving her car because the car died and had to be pulled up the last hill to the house."

Georgia backed away and went to see Sam. She returned with a key and handed it to Trace, but her eyes turned to Riley. "I'm glad you checked on her and came to help."

They took the key and went to the car. Trace tried to start it. After it refused, he opened the hood and leaned over the engine. Riley didn't have Trace's expertise with cars, so he stayed out of the way and waited, knowing Trace would ask for help if he wanted something.

"The fan belt's broken," he said after a few minutes. "I keep a spare in my truck, since the things break so often. She needs a new battery, but I don't have an extra one of those."

Riley doubted she would feel she could afford it, but he knew she would figure out a way to deal with the problem. When Trace got the car started a while later,

Riley got in the truck and waited for him to take the key back to Sam.

"Lily's birthday is Saturday," Trace said when he got behind the wheel. "Callie would love to have you come eat supper with us."

"I'm kind of old for a kid birthday party."

"But you're a kid at heart," he teased. "And Lily thinks you're the best *unkie* in the world."

Riley grinned. "She's my girl, but I don't want to intrude on your family time."

"Callie will be disappointed if you don't come." He backed out of the driveway. "I'd like you there, too."

That did it. He liked Trace. And, of course, he loved his sister. He just didn't like having them *take care* of him. "All right."

When Trace pulled in at the Blake house, Riley got out of the truck and started to close the door. Then he paused. "Did you by chance find out any more about what the school is going to do with their old piano?"

Trace grinned. "As a matter of fact, I did. Mom and Dad came to visit last night, and Mom said that they're going to offer it for sale."

"Did she say how much they're going to ask for it?"

"She mentioned five dollars."

"Thanks. I'll see you Saturday."

After Trace left, Riley went to work at the mill, but he couldn't get Jolene out of his mind. He kept an eye on the school, and when the students left at the end of their day, he shut down the saw and headed across the road.

Chapter 6

Jolene gathered her purse and the satchel of papers she meant to take home to finish marking. Georgia had already come in the buckboard and taken Kurt and Karen home.

"I'm finished, Miss Delaney," eighth grader Daniel announced, replacing the erasers after dusting them and washing the blackboard. "See you Monday."

She followed him outside and went to get her bike. She placed her bags in the basket in front of the handlebars and started to get on, but her eyes strayed to a strip of snow near the building that had not been trampled.

In an impulsive act, she leaned the bike against the steps and walked over to the clean snow. Then she fell backward onto it and began to sweep her arms up and down to create a snow angel. Then she got up and made another one. As she closed her eyes and formed a third, words burst from her mouth. "Thank you, Father, for

Your heavenly angels that provide unseen help when we need it."

A chuckle made her eyes pop open and her mouth go silent. She stared upward, and nearly fainted at the sight of Riley Blake watching her from a few feet away. She shot to a sitting position, her legs straight out in front of her, feeling silly.

"Are you saying you believe in angels?"

She stared at his frowning face.

"I do," she said firmly. "The Bible says there are angels, that God provides them to be unseen aid on our behalf."

Riley stared at her as if she were crazy. Then he shook his head. "You're one of a kind, Jolene Delaney. I think you get more religious all the time."

"I don't get more religious. I just reflect more on the promises of God. I wish..." She paused, and feeling the icy shield forming around him, she shivered and gathered her composure. "I assume you came over here for a reason."

"I came to tell you that your car is running again. Trace fixed it. I also wanted to tell you that he says the school is going to sell their old piano. They're asking five dollars for it."

How in the world could she come up with an extra five dollars? "Thank you for telling me about the piano, but how did Trace come to fix my car? Never mind," she said as she recalled seeing Riley talking to Kurt back by the pump yesterday. "Thank you for telling Trace. I'll settle up and thank him tomorrow."

On Saturday, Callie came up the steps onto the Delaneys' front porch, a twin in each arm, Lily trotting ahead of them.

"Lily has something to ask you," she said to Jolene, who stood at the door.

Jolene grinned, stooped and opened her arms. "What's on your mind, Lily?"

"Today is my birthday," she chirped as she ran into her embrace. "I want you to come eat birthday cake with me."

"I think I can do that." Jolene hugged the girl to her. How she loved this tiny, black-haired imp. Lily had stolen her heart at birth, and Callie knew it. Jolene suspected her friend of occasionally using Lily to manipulate her, like now. But she could not resist.

"Good, we'll expect you for supper. How's Sam?" Callie asked as she entered the house.

"Behaving better now that Georgia is around to keep an eye on him. His leg is still bad, but it's slowly improving."

Callie put the little boys down. "I heard about your new arrangement. I'm glad to hear he's on the mend."

The Sullivan children entered the living room and eyed the new arrivals. "Can they come play with us?" Nathan asked timidly.

"Sure," Callie answered, pulling the coat off a twin. As soon as she removed the second one, they scampered away. Lily watched them go, but hesitated to leave Jolene.

"It's okay, sweetheart. Go play with them." Jolene removed her own coat and smiled as Lily left.

"You have quite a family built up here," Callie said once they were alone and had cups of coffee to warm them. They could hear Georgia speaking to the children in the room down the hall.

Jolene sipped from her cup and set it on the table next to her chair. "It's making me lazy to have so much of the housework done."

"Enjoy it," Callie ordered. "You've worked so hard for so long that you don't know how to relax."

Uncomfortable, Jolene pushed a lock of hair behind one ear. "I'm still busy, just not so pushed for time. I need to speak to your husband," she said, diverting the subject. "He and Riley found out I had car trouble and fixed it."

"You can talk to him tonight." Callie's smile was satisfied, almost smug.

"Riley said the school is going to sell their old piano. Will you tell your mother-in-law that I want to buy it?"

Callie glanced around. "I assume Irene's gone to the church to play the one there."

Jolene nodded. "I don't know how I'm going to pay for it, but I've asked God to provide a way. Surely he wouldn't give Irene so much talent and never provide her with an instrument of her own."

"I'll tell Trace's mom."

"Can we hide it in the room where we have our swap meets? I'd like to give it to Irene for Christmas."

Callie's smile broadened. "That's a good idea. Do you still have feelings for Riley?"

Where had that come from so abruptly?

"I like him," she admitted carefully. "I think we can be friends."

"Dare I hope for more?"

"I don't think so." Even as she said it, her feelings intruded. This restlessness that had plagued her lately almost frightened her. She had given up her plan to marry a long time ago.

Callie studied her, and then a knowing smile crept across her face. But she said no more.

Riley's stomach knotted with uncertainty as he rode Daisy to his sister's house. While the mare clip-clopped along the road at a placid pace, he pictured Callie's family and the happiness she had found with Trace Gentry. Could he ever have that kind of relationship? He had not thought so for so long that the slight hope that had sneaked through him was puzzling.

When he rode up the lane to the house he had helped Trace build, he recognized Jolene's car parked in front of it and swallowed hard. Did she know he was coming?

No, he didn't think so. His sister and brother-in-law had probably arranged this little get-together, which should make him angry. But for some reason it only irritated him. He hitched Daisy to the gatepost and headed up the plank walkway that crossed the yard.

When he reached the porch, Lily's squeal erupted and the door swung open. "Unkie Wiley," she shouted, charging at him.

He swept her up in his arms, her exuberance erasing some of his tension. With her help, he would survive the evening. He hugged her and put her down.

"She loves it when you come," Callie said from the doorway. "Now get in here so I can shut the door. It's freezing."

Inside the house, pleasant aromas drifted from the kitchen. The sound of metal clanging on metal indicated cooking was still in progress. He scanned the room and didn't see Jolene, so it had to be her in the kitchen. Comfortable furniture occupied the room, a warm collection Callie had accumulated piece by piece since her marriage.

Jolene came to the doorway—and stopped abruptly when she saw him. No, she had not known he was coming. For sure, anyhow. For some reason it amused him that she could be manipulated as easily as he could. What did not amuse him was how good it felt to see her. With her hair pulled to her nape in a ribbon and hanging down her back, and her blue dress with a white collar framing her oval face, she looked natural and comfortable here in his sister's house.

A blush crept up her neck and brightened her face. "Hi, Riley," she greeted him briefly and escaped back to the kitchen. So what if he made her uncomfortable. That made them even.

Trace came from another room. "Glad you made it." He stuck out a hand.

Riley glared at him and ignored the hand. "You'll pay," he growled softly.

Trace's mouth gaped in mock horror. "You would take revenge on a guy who's married to your sister?"

"That doesn't give you permission to fool with me," he said.

Trace merely laughed. "I'll have Callie watch my back."

I could have cut more logs if I had stayed home. Winter is here and bad weather can't be far behind. Riley turned to leave, but couldn't do it. Lily might cry.

The food was good, and the cheery family atmosphere pleasant. The kitchen was roomy and orderly. A tall cabinet stood against one wall; a stove dominated the opposite one. What made him envious, though, was the refrigerator that stood in the corner of the room.

"You knew what you were doing when you built this house so close to town," he said.

Trace followed his gaze. "There was another location I liked, but we couldn't have had electricity out there."

"Having electricity is almost as good as being married," Callie said, putting her milk glass down. She aimed a sassy grin at Trace.

"Yeah. She only married me for a refrigerator and

lights." Trace did a poor job of looking and sounding gloomy.

"What I wouldn't give to have those things," Jolene admitted with a sigh of longing.

Trace dropped his poor-little-me expression. "I hope the Rural Electrification Administration will help rural homes and farms get electricity before long."

They discussed the matter at length. By the time Callie brought Lily's birthday cake, Riley had grown more comfortable and didn't feel quite so out of place. So had Jolene, judging by her chatty conversation.

"I'm four now, Unkie Wiley," Lily informed him, holding up four fingers. She shoved a big bite of cake into her mouth.

Next to her, Jolene grinned—and their eyes met. Their gaze held for a long moment before he looked away. Riley squelched the unwelcome urge to reach across the table and touch her hand.

"It's nice to be able to come over here like this and know Dad and Irene are not alone," she said. "Even if we don't have electricity, I think you all should come to Christmas dinner at our house this year."

"You have Georgia to help, and it would be easier on Sam," Callie said, looking over at her husband. "We could spend Christmas Eve with our parents."

"Sounds good to me." The loving look he gave her caused a funny feeling in Riley's insides. Envy?

"Will you bring your parents?"

Riley started when he realized Jolene's question was addressed to him. "If they haven't made other plans." He would talk to them as soon as he got home, find out their plans and divert them if possible.

"I have a dime," Lily squealed, holding up a coin she had taken from a gift package. "I can go to a picture show." She bounced out of her seat and rounded the table to Riley. "Will you take me, Unkie Wiley?"

He looked at Callie, then Trace. "I think your parents are the ones to do that."

Her lower lip stuck out, and she shook her head. "No, I want you to take me." She climbed up into his lap.

Callie shrugged at him. "She loves Mickey Mouse."

"Callie made the doll for her, and I gave her the dime for show fare," Trace explained. "But I can't figure out why she wants an ugly galoot like you to take her."

"I want Jolene, too," Lily declared.

Riley saw Jolene stiffen.

"You don't need me, sweetie." Her voice sounded strained.

Lily's head bobbed. "Yes, I do."

Jolene looked at Trace. "I haven't thanked you for fixing my car," she said in an obvious effort to change the subject.

"Glad we could do it."

"How much do I owe you?"

Trace's smile faded. "I don't want your money." Then he pursed his lips in thought. "I could use a favor, though."

"Name it."

His mouth twitched. "I've seen Mickey too many times. Take Lily and consider us even."

Riley snorted. Then realized that he was caught, too. He sighed in resignation.

Father, I'm trusting You for the money I need. Jolene prayed with one half of her brain while listening to a student read with the other half. At least the combination of teaching and praying kept her mind too absorbed to think about going to the Saturday matinee with Riley.

After school she went home earlier than usual. "I have to run some errands after I peek in on Dad," she explained to Georgia when she, Karen and Kurt entered the house.

"He had a pretty good day," Georgia called after her.

Jolene found Sam sleeping. Satisfied, she returned to the living room and started to go back outside, but paused when she spotted her name on an envelope lying on the lamp table. Dad must have had Georgia bring the mail in from the box at the road. She picked the envelope up and opened it.

"Thank you, Lord," she breathed when she found a two-dollar payment from the Grit publishers for the last article she had sent them. She tucked it in her purse and practically ran to the car. Her first stop in town was at the gas station.

"What can I do for you today?" Dave Freeman asked, leaning down to peek in her open window while wiping his hand on an oily rag.

"Do you still buy and resell bicycles?"

"Yep. I fix 'em or just spruce 'em up, whatever they need. Sometimes I even build one from parts I've saved from the ones beyond fixin'. You got one you want to get rid of?"

She nodded. "Yes. It's older, but in pretty good shape."

He tipped his head and readjusted his cap. "How much you askin' for it?"

"Three dollars."

He considered. "I've seen you ride it. Okay, bring it by."

"Is tomorrow after school okay?"

"That'll be fine."

She drove across town to the home of Trace's parents and gave Mrs. Gentry the two dollars from Grit, plus the three dollars from her purse that she had intended for groceries, to pay for the piano. She would replace the grocery money tomorrow after she sold the bike.

"When can you get it moved?" Mrs. Gentry asked.

"Would Thursday or Friday afternoon be okay?"

The prim, fastidiously groomed older woman nodded. "I'll tell the school board it'll be removed by the end of the week."

Jolene's last stop was to see Callie and tell her about the purchase.

"Trace and Dad will move it," Callie assured her. "I'll let you know which night as soon as I find out when they can do it."

With that settled, Jolene drove home. "Thank you, Father. Once again You have provided."

"You feel like helping me and Trace move a piano?" his dad asked Riley Tuesday afternoon as they positioned a log behind Daisy. "Callie came by and said Jolene bought one from the school and needs it moved. But she wants to put it in the back of the dealership so her little sister won't know about it."

Riley groaned silently and wrapped the ropes around the log. "That means moving it twice. But I admit it's a great idea for a Christmas present. When do you want to do it?"

"Trace says the best time for him is Thursday after work."

"She said she couldn't afford it. I wonder how she managed to buy it," Riley said to himself as much as to his dad.

"Callie said she got some money for a magazine article. And she sold her bicycle."

Riley's head jerked around. "She needs that bike. She

rides it to school when her car breaks down, which is way too often."

Arlie shrugged. "I guess she wanted the piano more."

Riley swallowed a lump the size of a walnut. In a caring and generous act she had sacrificed something of value to herself in order to give her sister a piano. How could he continue to resist her? Tentacles wrapped around his heart and squeezed until he could hardly breathe. He had to get out of here.

"Let's finish up here and go to supper."

The week sped by. They cut a lot of logs and moved the piano for Jolene. Riley worked hard and pushed thoughts of Saturday from his mind. By Friday morning he was able to make his early morning trip to the Delaney farm to milk and split a stack of wood without spending every moment thinking of Jolene. By the time he returned home, he felt he had his emotions under control.

"I miss Delmer." His dad yelled over the noise as he guided another log into the saw that was run by the gas-powered steam engine. His younger brother had developed into a much better worker after a near-fatal brush with a gangster several years before.

Riley took the newly ripped board and tossed it onto the growing pile. As he turned around, he saw an old Model T Coupe turn into their driveway and stop. Two men got out and headed toward the mill. A sick feeling curdled his insides as he recognized Troy and Chuckie Lonigan.

"Can we take a break?" he shouted over the noise of the saw.

Arlie looked past him, and frowned when he spied their visitors. He shut down the saw and walked away, his mouth set in a grim line that sent guilt spiraling through Riley.

"Heard you been back around," Troy said as he and his brother approached. "Thought it wuz time we stopped by to see you."

A lanky guy with unkempt brown hair and heavy brows that met over the bridge of his nose, Troy had been a classmate. Chuckie, two years younger, was short and stocky, with a mouth that revealed tobacco-stained teeth. Neither of them favored cleanliness.

"We missed you," Chuckie said.

"What are you up to these days?" Riley asked, uncomfortable but reluctant to be rude to his neighbors.

"Oh, we still sell a little hooch, and do some odd jobs."

At Troy's words, Chuckie's mouth formed a smirk. "We don't have to sneak around anymore since prohibition got repealed."

"We thought we could go hunting, or ride to town and hang out," Troy said.

Riley glanced up at the car by the house and realized it was the same one they had bought back when they were making good money. "I've got too much work to do," he hedged, hoping to beg off without offending them.

Troy's smile disappeared. "What's the matter? You got too good for us?"

Chapter 7

Riley knew he should avoid these two, but he didn't want to make enemies of them. That could be dangerous.

"That's nonsense," he denied. "We have to get enough lumber cut to build Mom and Dad a new house in the spring, and I don't know how long I can hang around here. I'll run out of money before long."

Troy's eyes shifted to the pile of boards behind them. "Me and Chuckie here don't know much about running that saw, but we can cut and skid logs. How's about we help you all day. Then we can go to town tonight."

Riley debated. He wasn't crazy about having these two around, and he knew his dad would not like it, but they sure could use the help. And they hadn't suggested anything bad.

"All right," he agreed uneasily. "I'll go tell Dad you'll help me in the woods and he can work here at the mill today."

Surprisingly, Troy and Chuckie proved to be good help. They cut and skidded more logs that day than he and Dad could have done, proving that they could do honest work if they put their minds to it.

"We'll come back for you after supper," Troy drawled when they quit for the day. He headed for their old car, Chuckie trailing after him.

Riley put the tools away and turned the horses into the corral.

"I hope you know what you're doin'," his dad said as they walked to the house.

"I'm not sure I do, but I'd rather have them as friends than enemies. They were a good help today."

"Yeah, they were," Dad growled.

"All they're asking in return is that I go ridin' with 'em this evening. Surely there's no harm in that."

Arlie gazed up at the darkening sky. "I hope not. They got you involved in peddling their bootleg before, and you don't need any more trouble."

"I know."

Riley was still reminding himself of that when Troy and Chuckie returned an hour later.

"Whoo-ee, let's go have some fun," Troy howled from the car window as Riley met them in the drive.

Riley crawled into the backseat, thankful to not have to sit next to them. Chuckie not only reeked, but he took up so much space that Riley would have been squashed between them.

At the edge of town Troy drove past the jail and turned onto Main Street. Businesses lined the entire two blocks of it, all of which were closed except the ice cream parlor. The only life in the small town after six o'clock in the evening consisted of the people, like them, who cruised a path that began on Main Street, turned left at the ice cream parlor, took two more lefts and returned to Main Street. The outside air was cold enough to freeze their whiskers off, and cold leaked in through every crack and cranny of the old car, so it wasn't much warmer inside it. The purpose of all this was basically to check out the girls and kill time.

Riley enjoyed the chance to ride something other than a horse or buckboard, but he was miserably cold and felt self-conscious about being seen with these guys. Their family had never run much of a farm, being too slipshod in their methods and work habits—when they worked.

By the end of an hour he wished they would tire of the pointless driving and head home. He was about to suggest it when the car began to sputter.

"Shucks." Troy slapped his hands against the steering wheel. "Guess we're out of gas." He pulled to the curb and stopped just as the motor died.

"Sit tight." Troy looked back at Riley and reached over the seat to lift the gas can and hose from the rear floorboard. When he got out of the car, Chuckie did the same.

"Be right back."

Together the brothers strode off up the street. As Riley realized what they were up to, he breathed a sigh of thankfulness that they hadn't asked him to go along. He slunk down in the seat, wishing he were invisible as the marshal drove up the street. Troy and Chuckie had not changed. They were siphoning gas from parked cars.

Minutes later, they returned, swaggering and laughing. They poured a full can of gas into the tank and crawled back into the car.

"This old thing can still run a race," Troy bragged as he revved the motor and pulled into the street. "I bet it could still outrun either one of them old nags you ride." He aimed the challenge over his shoulder at Riley.

Chuckie snapped his fingers. "Let's have a race." He twisted around in the seat. "You afraid to put one of your horses up agin' it?"

Riley shook his head. "I don't think I should. They put in a lot of hard work and deserve to rest at night."

"So let's do it this weekend," Chuckie persisted.

"I don't think so."

He was relieved when they didn't push further.

Jolene packed a lunch for three—rather, two and a half—and wrapped it in a bread wrapper. "I'll be home around two," she informed Irene as she put on her coat.

"Dad and I will be fine. Don't worry about us," Irene responded with a wave of her hand.

"If I'm late you can start supper. I'll help when I get home."

"Yes, Mama." Irene gave her a saucy grin. "Now go get Lily and Riley and have fun. That's an order."

Jolene rolled her eyes and opened the door. "Don't…"

"Go." Irene pointed a finger at the door.

Jolene went. Some "date" this was. She drove to the Blake house and got Riley, who didn't seem overjoyed when he got into the car. It probably offended his masculinity to have to accept a ride from a woman. Especially her. Too bad.

"Are you not speaking to me?" she asked when they were halfway to Callie's house and he hadn't uttered a word.

He shrugged. "Got nothing to say. We both got finagled into this."

"So you're just making the best of it."

"I guess."

Well, if he didn't want to talk, that was fine with her. But that changed when they got to the Gentry home. Callie came to the door with Lily, and the little girl broke into a run toward them. When Riley opened the car door, she launched herself at him. "Unkie Wiley, Unkie Wiley," she chanted as he caught her in his arms. "Aunt Lily is coming for Chwistmas."

"That's the aunt you're named after?" Jolene asked the little girl.

Lily nodded vigorously. "Yes, she's my aunt Lily. She lives in Spwingfield, and she doesn't got any cows."

"Oh, she doesn't, does she?" Riley's chest quivered. "Maybe that's because she lives in the city."

Lily's head bobbed.

Riley nuzzled her neck and hugged her to his chest. "You may be named after your aunt Lily, but you're the spittin' image of your mother."

"No, no, no." Lily waggled a finger at him.

He frowned in puzzlement.

"Spittin' is yucky."

Jolene clamped her jaws together as Riley nearly choked on a laugh.

"You're right, sweetie, it's yucky. But you're not yucky," he managed to say.

"I know." She spread her little palms.

Callie leaned over and aimed a smug grin at them. "She's all yours. Thanks for giving us a break. I hope you survive." Rubbing her arms, she turned and ran back into the house.

Riley closed the door, and Jolene put the car in motion. Lily, full of vim and vigor, chattered all the way to the movie house.

"Who would have thought the Saturday-morning matinee would be so popular," Riley drawled as they joined the line in front of the building.

"I think there are people who use it as a babysitting service."

His laugh was a deep, pleasant sound that made Jolene's heart leap into her throat. He didn't laugh nearly enough.

As they got near the ticket booth, Riley stooped over and removed the knotted handkerchief that Callie had pinned to Lily's dress. He took her dime from it and placed it in her tiny hand. "Here you go, Squirt."

The squirt grinned at him. "Thank you, Unkie Wiley. Now I can pay the lady."

"Yes, you can." He picked her up so she could put her dime on the ledge of the booth. When he put her down, he reached into his pocket.

"I'll pay for us," Jolene said, opening her purse.

He turned a fierce scowl on her. "You will not."

"But you don't have a job right now."

"I've got a few pennies saved up."

"Then pay for yourself, but not for me."

His mouth tightened further. "You drove. I pay."

Seeing that he would not be swayed, she closed her purse.

Inside was bedlam. They joined the mob in the lobby that consisted of more kids than adults and worked their way inside the theater. Riley carried Lily to prevent her being run over. Watching his treatment of his small niece endeared him to Jolene more than ever.

"This is fun," Lily prattled as they found three empty seats together and slid into them. She wiggled around onto Riley's lap and got right up in his face, eye to eye. "I wuv you, Unkie Wiley."

"I love you, too, Squirt. Do you want to sit over here?" He patted the empty seat beside him. "Or do you plan to sit on me the whole time?"

She giggled. "I want to sit on you."

Riley darted a look over at Jolene. "I guess I've got an anchor."

"A sweet one." She reached over and brushed flyaway strands of silky hair away from Lily's face.

"You're just jealous," he accused.

Her mouth dropped open. "In your dreams."

He chuckled. "Oh, yeah."

Lily stood on his thighs so she could see better, her little head turning in a slow scan of the room.

"Lots of kids come to see Mickey," she observed. Suddenly, she spun back around to face Riley and Jolene and sat down, her little face wrinkled. "Where are your kids?"

They exchanged puzzled glances. "We don't have any kids," Riley explained.

"Why?"

"Uh, we're not married."

Jolene had to cover a smile with her hand, even while her heart thumped crazily.

"Why?"

Her smile dissolved. She directed her eyes forward.

Fortunately, the lights dimmed at that moment, distracting Lily from her question. She whirled around, her eyes instantly riveted to the screen. Thankfully.

Riley leaned over and whispered in Jolene's ear, "Nosy kid. Next time you get to answer her questions."

Lily sat in rapt attention through the cartoon. When a newsreel began, she leaned back into Riley's chest and once again surveyed her surroundings. But she remained quiet.

The short subject, an episode of *Our Gang*, held her attention. During the *Rin Tin Tin* serial she snuggled up to Riley and put her arms around his neck.

Halfway through the feature, a Shirley Temple movie,

the picture flickered and went off. When people began to clap and stomp, Lily stood up on Riley's thighs. "Feed it a nickel. Feed it a nickel," she shouted.

Jolene and Riley both laughed.

"She's obviously heard that before," Jolene said in his ear. Her throat tightened. Being here with him made her happy—but scared. If only he were a Christian. If only... She inhaled deeply and shut down the thoughts.

She opened the bread wrapper and took out the sandwiches. "Here, we may as well make use of this time to eat. It's lunchtime."

The movie came back on while they ate, and quiet was restored in the theater. When it ended, Lily resumed her chatter. Jolene stuffed the empty wrapper in her purse.

"I think she talked my ear off," Riley said after they had returned Lily to her parents and headed home. He pulled on his lobe.

"You love her."

"Yeah. I enjoyed taking her to see Mickey."

Silence fell, and stretched, as Jolene drove. When she pulled in at his house, she wasn't sure what to say.

Riley placed his hand on the door handle. "Thank you for keeping me and Lily company. This is all backward, you know."

She frowned. "What's all backward?"

"I should be picking you up and taking you to the picture show, not you driving me around."

She shrugged. "I happen to have a car. You happen to have the cutest and smartest niece in the country. I don't know about you, but I had a good time."

He grinned. "Me, too. So much I'd like to do it again sometime—without Lily."

Jolene gave a nervous laugh. "That's probably not a good idea."

"Yeah, I guess you're right." He got out of the car and leaned down, his smile fading. "See you around."

With her hands trembling, Jolene backed up and drove away.

Riley stopped in the house only long enough to get a drink of water. Then he went out the back door and joined his dad at the woodpile. He grabbed an ax and began to split the four-foot log chunks into pieces that would fit in the stoves.

After supper he considered cutting more wood, but decided it was getting too dark.

"What's the matter, son? You seem restless."

He turned from staring out the window to face his dad. "I guess I am. I think I'll saddle Baldy and go for a ride."

Dad gave him a knowing grin. "Got business over around the Delaney farm?"

Riley shook his head. "I may ride into town."

It was a cold ride, with the temperature below freezing, but it helped keep his mind from being too active. He gazed at the stars in the black sky and saw no sign of snow or sleet. But that could change within minutes.

About a mile from the city limits he steered the gelding onto a well-used side road that was a shortcut. He passed the icehouse and turned in at the rear of the gas station that was located on the corner of the block, across the road from the ice cream parlor. Signs on the side of the building advertised car parts and five-cent soda pop.

"Well, howdy, Riley," Dave Freeman, an old friend and classmate, greeted him, the gap between his front teeth flashing. "I'm sorry, but I can't gas up what you're riding."

Riley slid to the ground and stuck out a hand. "Good to see you again."

"What's on your mind?" Dave asked after they shook hands.

Not quite sure how to phrase his question, Riley hesitated. "I believe you bought a bicycle from Jolene Delaney earlier this week."

"Sure did." He pulled a grease rag from his hip pocket and wiped his hands. "You interested in the bike or the gal?"

"Do you still have the bike?" He ignored the reference to Jolene.

"Sure do. You wantin' to buy it?"

"If I can."

"Not much money, huh?"

"Not a lot."

Dave's lips pursed and squiggled around. "How much firewood you give me for it?"

"Two buckboard loads?"

Dave rubbed his chin. "Make it three and it's yours."

"Sold. When do you want your wood?"

Dave shrugged. "When you can get it cut."

"I'll get on it next week. I'd like to have the bike in time for Christmas."

Dave fluttered a hand in dismissal. "Pick it up anytime. I know you'll deliver. Does this mean you finally mean to court that girl properly?"

"We're just friends."

Dave snorted then laughed as heat crept up over Riley's face. "You don't have anyone. Neither does Jolene. You need each other. And I think you'd make a good match."

"If you say so." Riley didn't have the energy to argue with him. "Thanks. Is it okay if I hitch Baldy to your garage door while I walk down to the drugstore for an ice cream?"

"Sure."

As he walked down the street, Riley felt pleased with the bargain he had made. But he didn't know how to give the bicycle to Jolene. Considering their history, he hesitated to present it directly to her. He would do it anonymously, he decided.

Lost in thought, he didn't notice the marshal until they came face-to-face under a streetlight.

Leon dipped his head. "Hello, Riley. How you doing these days?"

"Okay, I guess."

"I was surprised to see you with the Lonigan brothers last night."

"It was a mistake. But they're my neighbors, and they helped me cut logs all day yesterday. Running around with them for a bit seemed like a small trade-off. No more, though."

"If you mean that, you should tell me anything you know about their shenanigans."

"You're putting me in kind of a tight spot, Leon."

The marshal's look pierced him. "I see what you mean. But you can't turn a blind eye if they're stealing."

Riley looked up into the glare of the streetlight. How much should he say?

"You're not being a rat if you help stop crime."

He met Leon's eyes and swallowed. "I think they're siphoning gas from parked cars."

Leon nodded and grimaced. "I figured it was them. I've been getting reports for some time, but it's gotten worse lately. Any idea what else they got going?"

Riley raked his teeth over his lower lip. "I saw some feathers in the back floorboard. Could mean they're stealing chickens."

Leon drew a long breath. Then his expression turned

speculative. "Why don't you hang around with them a little more?"

Now it was Riley's turn to speculate. He didn't like the feel of this. "Why?"

The marshal gave him a frank appraisal. "I have an even bigger problem than missing gas and chickens. Several cars have been stolen in recent months."

Riley took a step back. "And you think Troy and Chuckie are doing it?"

"I suspect them, but I can't prove it. I need to find out where they're storing them and who they're selling them to. I can't get close to them without spooking them into hiding. But you could. They trust you."

So what does that make me?

"I know what you're thinking," the marshal went on. "You think it would be two-faced to act like their friend and snitch on them. But think how it would make you feel if you had a car and they stole it."

"You know how to push the guilt buttons, don't you?"

"Whatever it takes."

Riley considered the angles. Leon had left him alone after he'd been shot five years ago. Probably figured he had been punished enough and wouldn't peddle any more moonshine for the Lonigans. Leon had been right. He was probably right now, as well. Riley owed the man.

"What do you want me to do?" His words came out like a snarl.

"Just spend time with them. Keep your eyes and ears open and let me know if you find out anything useful."

Resignation settled over him. "All right."

"Thanks. I'll keep your name out of it." He touched the brim of his hat and moved on up the street.

Riley didn't enjoy his ice cream all that much. His stomach rolled and tumbled as he rode Baldy home.

When he reached the house, he rode on past it, but slowed the gelding's pace to a walk. How could he have gotten into this situation?

He rode up to the Lonigan house and dismounted. The place was as trashy as ever. An assortment of junk cluttered the yard and porch. The house had several cracked windows and tattered screens.

As he hitched Baldy to a tree, Troy opened the door and came outside. "What you doing over here this late? Is something wrong?"

Riley forced a grin. "Nope. I just got to thinking and decided to take you up on that race. Daisy's older and not so fast, but Baldy here can run circles around that rattletrap of yours."

Chapter 8

As they got ready for church the next morning, Jolene marveled at how fast Georgia Sullivan and her little brood had become a part of the household. Georgia was skilled at nursing care and good at cooking, mending and housekeeping, anything that needed doing. She was also becoming a good friend.

"You're spoiling us, Georgia," she accused as they cleared the breakfast table. Georgia had already helped Sam to and from the table and gotten her children ready for church. "I wish you would go to church and let me stay with Dad."

Georgia smiled at her. "It's best I stay this week. Maybe next week we'll switch. Or Sam might be ready to go with us. Are you sure you don't mind taking all the kids?"

Jolene placed her hands on her hips and produced a

mock glare. "Haven't you figured out yet that I'll go to great lengths to get my hands on small children?"

The woman laughed, the first time Jolene could remember hearing her do so. "You sure do like kids. I don't see how you can want mine with you so much when you've already spent the whole week working with other people's kids. You should have a whole passel of your own."

Her hand flew over her mouth. "I'm sorry. I hope I didn't say something hurtful."

Jolene forced a smile. "The Lord hasn't seen fit to give me a husband and children. I guess He has other plans for my life, like taking care of the kids of other people. Thank you for letting me enjoy yours."

She opened the door for Karen and Kurt to lead their younger siblings outside. Irene had already gone to the car and started it—anxious to start driving. She was growing up too fast.

Thirty minutes later Jolene relaxed in the pew in the back of the Deer Creek Mission where her Sunday school class met. Located about a mile from the Deer Creek School, the white-frame church had been built when she was a young girl. Her mind drifted.

It troubled Jolene to think about Irene growing up and leaving home. She was so pretty and talented, and the boys had already started competing for her attention. Was it Jolene's lot to be left a lonely old maid, to live out her life there on the farm, just her and her dad?

Following that thought came an image of Riley. He was handsome and caring. He was the son of a poor farmer with few prospects of ever being well-off, but that didn't matter to her. She had no aspirations to marry a rich man. A poor man would suit her fine, if she knew beyond a shadow of a doubt that he loved her—and that he was a Christian.

But she didn't need to be thinking about a relationship with any man. Her girlhood dreams that centered on Riley were over. She had her dad to think of, and a few more years with Irene. She must be content.

Noise from outside the building caught her attention. A car roared past the church, as did the pounding hooves of a galloping horse. The sounds faded, but then she heard yelling and a racing car coming from the clearing at the south side of the church. Who would be making all that racket on a Sunday morning during church?

When Sunday school dismissed, Jolene wasn't the only one who went to the door to look out. "What's going on?" she asked Pastor Jacob Denlow, who stood in front of her.

Her middle-aged, slightly balding pastor looked back at her and grimaced. "I'm not sure, but I sure hope it stops before service starts."

As Jolene peeked out the doorway, a car came roaring up the road from the opposite direction, a big red horse running alongside it.

"They're racing," the pastor said in amazement. "It's the car against the horse."

Jolene went rigid as she recognized the rider on the horse. She felt like she had been punched in the stomach. Disbelief brought tears to her eyes. Riley Blake couldn't be running around with the Lonigan brothers again. Hadn't he learned his lesson years ago?

As the car and horse sped on down the road out of sight, she spun and hurried back into the church. Thank goodness his parents were not here today.

"What was that?" Irene asked as she ushered the children into their pew.

Jolene took a couple of short, quick breaths before she

could speak. "Just some rowdies racing a horse against a car. Here, Nathan, you sit this side of me." She picked Nola up and set her on the other side. Karen and Kurt each sat by a younger sibling.

Irene hesitated, clearly wanting to ask more, but then she turned and went to the piano.

Lord, help me get through to Riley. He needs You in his life.

Oooga! Oooga!

The raucous car horn outside, accompanied by whooping and yelling, interrupted her silent prayer and half-formed plan to confront Riley.

The car passed beyond hearing range. Then it came roaring back, and the racket was louder. But there was no sound of a horse. Riley must have gotten into the car with them. Despair ate at Jolene.

The song service ended, and Irene came to sit with her and the children. At first Jolene was too distracted to absorb the pastor's message. But the story he was telling finally caught her attention.

"A boy wanted his dog to drink cod liver oil so it would have a more healthy and shiny coat. Every day he forced the stuff down the dog's throat. One day the bottle tipped over, and the boy went to get a rag to clean up the mess. Imagine his surprise when he got back and found the dog lapping up the spilled cod liver oil like he loved it."

Jolene wasn't sure she saw the point.

"Sometimes we use a similar method when we tell others about Christ. We share the gospel, but we are overly enthusiastic and end up alienating people instead of winning them."

Another passing of the car drew all eyes to the windows. The pastor paused, but continued quickly. "It's not our job to try to convict someone of sin. That's God's responsibility. We must tell others about Christ, but be sensitive, know when to back away and let God do the rest."

She closed her eyes and let the words seep through her. *Okay, Lord, he's in Your hands. Please draw him to You.*

After a restless night, Riley rose before dawn and rode Baldy to the Delaney farm. No more snow had fallen during the night, but drifts from earlier in the week still covered the grass and clogged the roadside ditches.

Regret ate at him about yesterday's events. When Troy and Chuckie said to meet him Sunday morning, he had not realized they would create so much racket and disturb people during church. He feared that the church people— including Jolene—had recognized all three of them.

When he arrived at the Delaney home, he dismounted and unhooked the lantern from the saddle horn. Sam met him at the door, balanced on his crutches, a milk pail dangling from the fingers of one hand.

"What do you think you're doing?" Riley darted a look behind them, hoping he would not have to face Jolene.

"I aim to milk," Sam declared. "Don't you give me any guff about it." He moved forward.

Riley darted over and helped the stubborn man down the steps rather than let him fall.

"Make him be careful and don't let him do too much."

The voice made Riley jerk his head up. He was relieved to find Georgia Sullivan in the doorway rather than Jolene.

He took the milk pail she held out to him, and then took the one dangling from Sam's hand. "I'll carry these. You concentrate on walking."

"There's a damp cloth in the one I gave you," Georgia called as they walked away. Then the door slammed shut.

Riley accompanied Sam to the barn and helped him maneuver through the doorway with his crutches. Then he set the milking stool beside one of the two jerseys they milked regularly.

Sam leaned his crutches against the stall and sat on the stool, his injured leg stuck out to one side. He took the wet cloth from the milk pail and washed the cow's udder. Then he put his head against her side and began to milk. "Run on and split the wood. I can handle this," he ordered without looking up.

Riley kept his back to the house as he worked at the woodpile. He didn't relax until he heard the car start and drive away and knew that Jolene had left for school.

Minutes later Sam hobbled from the barn. "I set the milk buckets by the far door and turned the cows into the lot."

Riley swung the ax and split a piece of firewood off a big chunk of log. Then he put the ax down. "It's good to see you up and around, Sam. But don't overdo. Okay?"

Sam grinned and leaned forward on the crutches. "Don't get bossy with me, boy. I appreciate the way you've helped out, but I need to get back to work, take care of my own chores so you can take care of yours. It felt good to get out this morning."

"Glad you're healing. But don't rush it. I'll keep coming while you ease back into your routine."

"You're a good man, Riley. There was a time when I worried about you. But you've put some bad things behind you and become a good man."

Sam's look of approval made Riley's insides squirm a bit. "I made mistakes. Some people never let me forget."

"But you've not let that beat you down. There was a time when I thought you and my daughter might be planning a future together."

Riley drew a deep breath and gripped the ax handle so tight he feared he might break it. "I had some hopes along that line," he admitted in a voice weak from strain. He never talked about those times. "It didn't work out."

Sam studied him from beneath shaggy, white brows. "I don't know what came between you, but if you ever want to talk about it, I'm a good listener."

Riley liked Sam Delaney, always had. But he couldn't see himself talking to Sam about his feelings toward the man's daughter. It puzzled him that a smart man like Sam would feel kindly toward him.

"God loves you, son. I hope you know that. I know you're not a real talker and especially might not want to talk to me. But you can always talk to God about anything—and anyone."

Every muscle in Riley's body tightened. "I guess God's out there, but I've never seen that he had time for a nobody like me."

"That's not true, Riley. He cares about every single human being he ever created, including you. The Bible says in First Peter that he doesn't want anyone to perish but all to come to repentance."

How had this simple conversation become a sermon? "So why did he let my brother die in that accident? Why have my parents had such a hard life?"

Sam rolled his head in a back and forth motion. "I don't know why things happened the way they did. But I know God cares about you and your family. I hear bitterness in you, and that's not good. It will eat you alive if you let it."

His insides churning, Riley put the ax down. "I guess he gave me two good hands to take care of myself with. And I need to get to doing that." He picked up the splitting wedge and maul and positioned the wedge on the wood.

"Think about it. I'll be praying for you." With that, Sam headed into the house.

Riley split that piece of wood and went to get the milk. When he finished Sam's chores, he went home to cut more wood, some for his family, and some for Dave Freeman.

Jolene looked out the windows at the light snow that drifted past the glass panes. She closed the book on the history lesson she had been discussing with the older students and addressed the entire classroom.

"I know most of you want to go outside in the snow, but it's too cold to stay out very long. So let's eat lunch at our desks, and then go out for a short recess."

She got no objections. So much for the art of compromise.

"The fire's getting low, Miss Delaney. And the wood box is about empty."

She looked at Jerry Bixby. He was right about the fire, but she strongly suspected he wanted to go after wood for other reasons. He had too much talent for trouble to be trusted out of the building alone.

"Thank you, Jerry. As soon as we eat our lunches and go out for recess, a couple of you older boys can fill the woodbox. Why don't you put the last sticks in the stove now?"

He frowned in disappointment, but did as she said. With trouble averted, Jolene sat at her desk and took her own lunch from the drawer where she stored it.

Kurt raised a hand in the signal that meant he needed to go to the privy. She nodded permission and he left.

Within minutes everyone finished eating, and they

went outside. Jolene stood on the steps where she had a good view of the entire front school yard and kept an eye on her students. She was shivering from the cold and considered ordering them inside when the sight of a buckboard coming across the road drew her attention. She stiffened when she recognized Riley on the seat. Her anger at him flooded back.

He pulled up by the woodpile and stopped. Then he hopped to the ground and loped around the side of the building. He returned moments later, with Jerry Bixby gripped by the shoulder and arm. He marched the boy up to the steps.

"I saw Mr. Bixby back there," he explained in a tightly controlled voice. "He was bullying the Sullivan boy and pushed him down. He had shoved his face in the ground and was telling him to go back to the town school when I pulled him off."

Jolene's temper flared. She hated that having Kurt and Karen staying with her and coming to school with her seemed to have caused jealousy in a few of the students.

She directed a withering look at Jerry. "Since you have so much energy, you may stay after school and clean the ashes from the stove. There's plenty more work you can do, as well."

Jerry jerked his arm free and glowered at her. "Your little sissy boy needs to work, too. Or do you take care of him like a baby?"

"Kurt works plenty, not that it's any of your business." She turned to face the rest of the students. "We're all going inside now, except Daniel and Virgil. They may each go get an armload of wood."

Jerry stomped inside just as Kurt came around the corner of the building. He looked rumpled, but not hurt. Jolene breathed a sigh of relief.

"I saw that your woodpile is getting low," Riley said as students filed past them into the building. "I didn't want them to get cold, so I brought a load."

His tone and phrasing made it clear to Jolene that his concern was for the students, not her. She appreciated his help, but she couldn't escape the image of him running around with the old friends who had gotten him into trouble before. "Thank you," she muttered as politely as she could. Then she turned and followed the students inside.

It snowed off and on all week. Riley thought his arms were becoming an extension of the ax handle. He cut wood for Sam each morning. Then he cut wood for his own family when he got home. After working with his dad the rest of the day cutting, skidding and sawing logs, he cut extra wood meant for Dave Freeman. At least working himself into a stupor kept him too tired to lie awake nights thinking about Jolene.

"I think I'll ride over and visit with Callie and Trace," he said as he got up from the supper table Friday evening.

"Don't stay out too late," his mother cautioned. "That sky looks like we could be in for some bad stuff coming down." She coughed into her hand.

"Why don't you go on to bed and try to shake that cold," he countered. "You, too, Dad."

"Soon as I get the dishes done," his mom said. "I hope Clem remembers to help with chores at the Burtons."

His younger sister, Clementine, was spending the week with her fiancé's family in Salem. Riley hoped people weren't all getting sick over there, as well. He had to stay healthy.

"Take the buckboard and you can deliver the little table I made for the kids," Dad said. "I'll load it while you hitch the team."

When he got to his sister's house, Riley took the table from the buckboard and went to the door. He set it down and knocked.

Callie opened it, her red-rimmed eyes evidence that she had been crying. Wisps of hair straggled around her face. A crying twin clung to each side of her rumpled skirt.

Riley stepped inside, closed the door and pulled her to him. "What's the matter?"

"He's sick," she sobbed into his chest.

He pulled back enough to see her face. "Who's sick? Trace?"

She nodded and sniffled. "He's so sick, Riley. The doctor came out and gave me some medicine for him. He's too sick to swallow the pills. I have to dissolve them in water and trickle it down his throat a few drops at a time. I'm afraid to leave him."

"Mama. Mama." The twins cried in unison.

Riley released Callie, and they both picked up a baby. He patted Luke on the back and looked around for Lily. She lay on the sofa, staring over at them in an uncharacteristically lethargic way. He went to the sofa and squatted beside her, still patting the baby.

"Are you okay, sweetheart?"

Her face scrunched up and she covered it with her hands. "My daddy's sick," she sobbed. "I don't want him to be sick."

Riley's heart went out to the little girl, to all of them. Callie was frazzled, and the kids were scared. He had to do something.

"Pack a bag for these three," he ordered, turning to face Callie. "I'll take them with me so you can concentrate on taking care of Trace. And please try to get a little rest so you don't collapse."

Callie frowned. "You can't do that."

He gave her a stern look. "Don't you think I'm capable of taking care of them?"

A slight twitch tugged at the corners of her mouth. "I think you can do whatever you set your mind to, big brother."

"Good. They need to be away from here, anyhow. The flu is contagious."

Her face paled. "Don't remind me. I've not been letting them into the room with Trace for fear they'll catch it. That's why they're so scared."

He put his twin on the sofa next to Lily. "You pack some clothes for them while I bring in the table I left outside your door. Dad sent it."

Callie wilted, no arguments left.

A few minutes later they bundled the children up in their coats and took them to the buckboard. Riley placed the twins on the floor below the seat and placed a thick blanket over them. Callie put Lily on the seat beside him and wrapped a quilt around her. Then she gave each of them a hug and a kiss. "Be good for Uncle Riley."

As he drove home, the responsibility he had just undertaken nearly overwhelmed Riley. Then another scary thought hit him. Mom and Dad were coughing and sneezing and not feeling well. They had no business taking care of three babies. They would do it, of course. But they needed to take care of themselves. And there was the risk of giving the kids their colds. What could he do?

He needed help. He knew Irene Delaney did some babysitting. He pulled in at the Delaney farm. As he did, the twins woke up and started to cry again. That set Lily to crying also. Panic seized him.

"Come on, kids. Let's go." He jumped to the ground

and set Lily down beside him. Then he reached over the side of the buckboard and scooped up the twins.

The front door opened as he made his way to the steps with his loud crew of crying babies.

"What in the world is going on?" Jolene demanded, coming out onto the porch.

Chapter 9

Jolene suppressed a giggle at the sight of Riley Blake loaded down with little ones, blankets trailing behind him, and Lily clinging to his leg.

He began to speak when he reached the steps. "Trace has the flu, and Callie is done in. I took the kids. Mom and Dad aren't feeling well, so I was wondering if Irene would consider some babysitting."

At his words all amusement fled. "Get in here." She pointed at the door.

He mounted the steps and stamped snow off his boots before entering the house. As soon as he had crossed the threshold with the twins, Jolene took Lily's hand and shut the door.

Both tiny boys wiggled until Riley had to put them down.

Irene came from the kitchen, and her dad clunked down the hall from his bedroom.

"What have we here?" Sam asked with a grin.

Irene grabbed a twin as he darted past her. "Looks like an invasion of tiny people."

Riley repeated his explanation.

"Have they eaten?" Sam asked.

A frown crossed Riley's face. "I didn't ask. I just took 'em and headed for home."

"We had soup," Lily informed them.

"Callie probably tried to get some down Trace," Jolene theorized. "Would you like a cookie?" she asked Lily.

The little girl's head bobbed as she practically shouted, "Yes."

"Cookie. Cookie," the twins chanted.

"Come with me." Irene headed to the kitchen, all three children trailing behind her.

Jolene wasn't sure what to do, so she took the blanket and quilt from Riley and began to fold them.

"Have a seat, Riley." Sam pointed a crutch at the sofa.

Riley shook his head. "I need to get on home. I wondered if Irene could go with us and help take care of these rascals. I don't know much about doing that."

Jolene fought to keep a straight face. That was obvious. She placed the bedding on a chair. "We have more room here, and none of us is sick. Why don't you leave them with us?"

He glanced toward the kitchen. "I can't do that. I told Callie I'd take care of them."

"Then stay here with them," Sam said. He eased into an overstuffed chair, his leg stiff in front of him.

Jolene swallowed in surprise. It was the sensible solution, but having Riley under their roof overnight was another matter.

Riley surveyed the room and beyond. "You already

have extra people staying with you. You don't need us underfoot."

"Georgia took her kids back to her sister's for the weekend. They won't be back until Sunday evening." Now why had she joined the effort to convince him?

Irene and the kids returned to the room, each child munching on a cookie. "I can ride my bike over and tell your folks you won't be in tonight."

"The boys can sleep in the bed Georgia normally uses," Jolene offered. "And Lily can sleep with Irene."

"Guess that leaves the sofa for you," Sam told Riley with a grin.

Riley glanced from one to the other of them, clearly uncertain what he should do.

"I'll go let your parents know not to worry." Irene went to get her coat.

"It's decided," Sam said.

Riley heaved a sigh of resignation. "Okay, we'll spend the night. But you may regret it."

Jolene's heart swelled. "No way. Callie's my best friend. I love her kids as much as if they were my own. We're pleased to be able to help her."

Irene left, and Lily crawled up into Jolene's lap. As they snuggled against her, the twins toddled to Riley. He removed his boots and took the boys to the sofa. He balanced one on each thigh, cookies and all.

Jolene sat in a chair facing him, her face going somber. "How bad is Trace?"

He cuddled the babies to him. "I don't know. I guess I was afraid to ask."

Memories of the 1918 flu epidemic that had killed millions hovered between them.

"I'll be praying that Trace doesn't have the Spanish kind of flu."

"Trace is strong," her dad said with confidence. "Give him a couple of days in bed with Callie's care and he'll beat it."

Jolene hugged Lily to her and met Riley's eyes, but neither of them said anything more. She watched his patience with the little boys and thought what a good dad he would be. She mentally shook herself and got up with the drowsy little girl.

"I'll put this one to bed."

When she had Lily tucked away and returned to the room, her dad had turned on the radio to listen to the *Grand Ole Opry*. Riley held two dozing babies.

"Give me one." She extended her arms.

He shifted forward and eased a twin toward her. Then he got to his feet and followed her to the bedroom where the little boys would sleep.

"They look so quiet and sweet," she observed as they placed them side by side.

"They're only quiet when they're asleep. I'll run back to the buckboard and get the bag Callie packed for them. I forgot it earlier."

"Feed your horses before you turn them into the corral," she said. "I assume you know how to find everything in the barn by now."

A low chuckle came from him. "I guess I do." He headed outside.

A couple of minutes later Jolene undressed the boys and maneuvered them in the little nightshirts from the bag Riley dropped next to her. Then she went back to the sleeping Lily, slipped off her clothes and put a nightgown on her. As she returned to the living room, Irene came through the door.

"I don't think Mr. and Mrs. Blake have the flu. It's just a cold. Dessie insisted she wants to take care of them tomorrow. I'll go help her." She gave a flip to the scarf she pulled from around her neck.

Sam turned off the radio. "I'm going to bed. You two can stay up all night if you want."

"I think I'll turn in, too," Irene said as she hung her coat on the hall tree.

As Sam left the room, Irene sidled over near Jolene and whispered in her ear, "Riley still likes you. I can tell." She ran down the hallway before Jolene could respond.

Jolene got a pillow and some bedding and brought them to the sofa. She put the pillow at one end and was spreading a quilt over the cushions when Riley returned from taking care of the horses. He took off his boots and set them outside on the porch.

"It's getting colder and snowing harder." He took off his gloves and blew on his hands.

Jolene frowned. "I hope it doesn't get so bad we can't get to church Sunday. There will be regular services in the morning and a Christmas program in the evening. Irene's involved in that."

He gave her an exaggerated look of amazement. "You mean you're not the one in charge of it?"

"Nope." She unfolded another quilt and gave it a flip to spread it over the first one.

"Where's everybody?"

"They're all in bed. The babies were already asleep when Irene got home. She and Dad both went to their rooms only minutes ago." She brushed the bedding to smooth it into place.

Riley sank onto the end of the sofa and reached up to clasp her arm. "Is Sam healing as well as he claims?"

The warmth of his hand made Jolene go still, even her eyes, as feelings surged through her in a powerful rush that was frightening. She didn't want to respond to him this way, but she didn't have the strength to prevent it. Her heart pounded, her poise gone.

"I think so," she croaked. "But even though he is, Georgia will stay here until the end of the school year so Kurt and Karen can attend our rural school. She'll spend at least part of the weekends at her sister's and…" She clamped her mouth shut to stop her babbling.

Riley pulled her down beside him and fastened his gaze on her, measuring, assessing. Jolene couldn't think clearly this close to him. The memories and emotions were too strong. She had known him as long as she could remember. Had gone to school with him and his siblings. Had become drawn to him as they grew older. Had been concerned about his continued refusal to let God control his life.

"The Sullivans are fortunate to have you taking care of them." An odd tenderness colored his voice. His eyes focused on her lips as he spoke.

"They're earning their keep," she assured him, hardly able to speak above a whisper as their faces inched close enough to feel his warm breath on her cheeks. Her reflection glinted back at her from his dark eyes.

His hand rose and brushed his knuckles across her cheeks, making her insides quiver. She stiffened her back, but didn't look away. Instead, she inventoried him—the brackets around his mouth, the crinkles at the corners of his eyes, his blue shirt that fit snug over arms made muscular by hard work. He was as attractive as ever. And just as wrong for her.

She swallowed as their faces inched even closer, his lips within a hairsbreadth of hers, and recognized the hard truth that, Christian or not, he still stirred strong feelings in her. Whether he wanted to or not, he felt something for her, too.

In a desperate grasp for sanity she sucked in a deep breath and said the first thing that came to mind. "I saw you outside the church Sunday morning."

He drew back, the mood broken like the snap of a twig. "I'm sure you drew your own conclusions." His deep voice vibrated with irritation.

Jolene inhaled quickly, wishing she could reclaim the words. "I reached no conclusion about how the race turned out."

Some of the tension eased out of him. If she was not mistaken, he came close to grinning. "Two races," he said drily. "We each won one. I quit while we were even."

"Just walked away and went home?"

His eyes narrowed. "Yes."

So he wasn't in the car with his friends after the race when they disturbed church service. Relief tempered the resentment she had harbored about the incident.

"It was a mistake to let them talk me into that race. It won't happen again."

Jolene raised a palm and got up. "I'm not preaching at you."

He leaned back and placed an arm along the back of the sofa. His silent stare made her uncomfortable.

She swallowed a lump in her throat. "I'm sorry if you feel that I preach at you. I've never meant to do that. I've taken a look at myself, though, and realized that my actions could possibly be taken that way. Forgive me. Good night."

She turned on her heel and practically ran from the room.

Riley woke before daylight and peered over the top of the sofa. Through the window he could determine that the snow had stopped. He had slept in his clothes, so he didn't have to get dressed. He stoked the coals in the fireplace and added wood to get the fire going. Then he got the milk buckets and put his shoes on before leaving the house. Out on the porch he pulled his rubber boots over his shoes and tramped through the fresh snow to the barn.

When he returned to the house with the milk, Irene met him at the kitchen door. Inside, he was greeted by the smells of bacon and the sounds of small humans anxious to eat.

"Jolene is changing the dressing on Dad's leg. I'll have breakfast on the table by the time you get that strained." Irene nodded to indicate the milk.

Lily climbed up on a chair and watched him strain the white liquid. Luke and Lane stood beside the chair. All three still wore their nightclothes.

"Mama. Mama," Luke whined.

"Mama's fine," Riley assured the child while guiding the stream of milk from the bucket into a crock Irene had provided. "We'll see her soon."

Lane took up the chant. "Mama." He rubbed his eyes and clutched Riley's leg.

"They're confused," Irene said from the stove where she was frying eggs.

Luke attached himself to Riley's other leg, making it almost impossible for him to move.

"If you'll bring me some small glasses, I'll pour some from this next bucket for these leeches," he said.

Irene turned and laughed at his predicament. "You do have a problem." She scooped the last of the eggs onto a platter, slid the skillet off the heat and went to get the glasses.

Riley filled them and then emptied the bucket into the crock. His eyes were only off the glasses for a moment, but during that time little hands reached up and grabbed the glass. The next thing he knew, Luke had pulled it off the table and tipped it into his face. He wailed and dropped the glass.

"My, my, what have we here?" Sam's voice boomed from the doorway.

Riley thumped the bucket onto the table and reached for the little boy. Panic hit him anew. He had no idea how to deal with such little ones. He put Luke on his shoulder and patted him. "It's okay, Luke."

Jolene appeared next to them. "Here, let me have him. Poor baby," she crooned as she transferred him to her shoulder, where he drooled onto her gray wool dress. "You're hungry and miss your mommy and daddy."

At mention of his parents, his face wrinkled and he began to cry in earnest. So did Lane.

"Oops, I shouldn't have said that. Let's go get you cleaned up."

Watching Jolene walk away with the child, Riley almost missed seeing Lane about to pull another glass off the table. He grabbed it just before it could topple. Then he sat in the nearest chair and boosted the child onto his lap.

"Here you go." He held the glass for Lane to drink. He knew this was Lane because of the small cowlick above his right eye.

"Lily and I will eat together." Irene sat beside the little girl.

"Guess I get to eat by myself," Sam declared, easing himself into a chair. "Sorry I didn't make it out to help you milk. That bossy girl of mine caught me and threatened to throw my breakfast out if I went out in the snow. She's afraid I'll fall." He snorted.

"Be glad she takes good care of you," Riley said with a grin. He put the milk glass down and scooted his chair closer to the table. He forked a tiny bite of egg from the plate Irene had put before him and poked it in Lane's mouth.

Jolene returned with Luke and sat at the vacant place next to Irene. Then she looked at her dad.

Sam bowed his head and said a blessing over the food, ending with, "Lord, we ask that You make Trace well. These little ones need him. We all do."

Riley's chest constricted. *God, if You're listening, please heal Trace.*

After breakfast, Jolene and Irene began the cleanup.

"I'll hitch the team and take this tribe off your hands."

Jolene stopped working and faced him. "We would love to keep them, but we understand. I'll get them bundled up and their things ready to go. Will you promise to bring them back if you need help? For any reason," she added with emphasis. "We care. And we'll be praying."

"I know." He was truly touched by the offer—and the caring. "Thank you for everything." Strangely reluctant to leave, he backed toward the door.

"As soon as we get the dishes done and some food fixed to take with me, I'm going to go see Callie," she said as he put his shoes back on to leave.

When he pulled the buckboard in at home a half hour later, his mother opened the door and peeked out.

"Don't come out in the cold," he called across the yard. "I'll bring them to you."

"Wait here, Lily," he instructed his niece. "I'll take Luke and Lane to your grandma and come back for you."

She turned her little face up and smiled at him. "Okay, Unkie Wiley."

Once he had all three kids and their belongings inside, he scrutinized his mother closely. "You look better today," he decided.

"I feel better." She paused in removing coats from the little ones. "I would have been fine last night. But I know how much Jolene loves Callie's kids. It's good we can share them."

Feeling better, Riley went back out to unhitch the team and feed them.

Sunday morning Jolene had just slid into a pew next to Dessie and Arlie Blake so she could help them with Callie's brood. She cringed when she heard the dreaded sound of a car approaching the church from a distance.

"What's going on?" Dessie asked when the car horn began to bleat, accompanied by loud whoops from two different voices.

Jolene hesitated to answer. "I assume it's the same rowdies who disturbed services last week."

Dessie eyed her intently. "Is it the Lonigan boys?"

"I'm afraid so."

"I'm glad Riley quit running around with them."

No way would Jolene mention seeing Riley with them last week.

The pastor approached, a hand extended as he circulated among the members, greeting them and shaking their hands.

Jolene waited until he had greeted the Blakes and Callie's children. "Can't anything be done about that?" she asked as the car passed the church again, the horn held down while the riders whooped and shrieked.

He shook his head. "I spoke to the marshal this week. He said he's sorry, but so long as nothing illegal has been done and they're not on church property, he can't do anything about it."

"Somebody oughta lock 'em in a room and beat on a dishpan till their eardrums pop." Arlie's words were sharp.

Pastor Denlow grinned. "We may have a rousing service today." He moved on.

The car made three more trips past the church before going away. Jolene did her best to concentrate on the message, but the noise, plus corralling Callie's little ones, made it difficult.

"I'll be happy to take them home with me," she said to Dessie when the service ended. She slipped Lily's coat over her arms.

Dessie patted her arm. "Thanks for the offer, but we'll be fine. You need to be free to go visit Callie and check on Trace."

Jolene smiled. "I'll be happy to do that."

But she didn't have to. As she and Irene cleaned up the kitchen after dinner, Callie drove up in front of their yard. She looked tired but wore a smile. Jolene ran out to meet her.

"I'm on my way to pick up the kids from Mom," Callie informed her. "Trace is doing much better, and I miss my babies."

Riley went outside after dinner and loaded the buckboard with wood from the pile he had cut for Dave. His mom and dad didn't hold with working on Sunday, but he didn't see delivering a load of wood as working. It was more like getting some exercise and going to visit a friend.

When he got back later that afternoon, he discovered that Callie had been there and taken her kids home. Hearing that Trace was recovering prompted him to drive his parents to church and slip into a back pew to watch the Christmas program. His eyes scanned the room and stopped at the sight of Jolene across the aisle and two pews up. His heart rate quickened and his vision danced as the lamplight spilled over her.

Irene began to play a piano introduction to the first song, and the program began. He forced his attention from Jolene onto the scene before him. As the children acted out the Christmas story, he enjoyed it more than he could have expected.

As it came to a close, his eyes were drawn back to the sheen of Jolene's hair. What would it feel like to hold her? Kiss her? The very idea made him feel as if he was falling.

When people stood for the benediction, Jolene turned slightly—and saw him. She went still for a moment before sending him a little smile that acknowledged his presence. Then she bowed her head.

After the prayer, people moved into the aisle and flowed toward the door. He should have moved faster, but he didn't. By the time he had exited the pew, Jolene had caught up to him. She kept her face aimed forward, looking anywhere but at him, until they reached the door. Then she turned and said, "It was good seeing you here." With that she gave a little wave and headed to her car in the opposite direction he was headed.

Which was how it should be.

They had nothing in common. Their lives were going in different directions.

He went to the buckboard and waited for his parents to join him. But he watched Jolene and Irene drive away, his traitorous eyes straining for a final glimpse as they drove out of sight.

Chapter 10

By midweek Riley was able to deliver a second load of firewood to Dave. Then Friday afternoon he took the last one. When he had it unloaded at Dave's house, he went to the station to claim the bicycle.

"It's in the shed behind the garage where I work on the bikes," Dave said, wiping his hands on the ever-present grease rag. He grinned at the team of horses and buckboard alongside his garage. "You need to get you a good used car so I can sell you gas."

Riley gave him a good-natured grin. "But you would expect me to pay for the gas. Maybe someday I'll find a decent job and get one."

Dave brushed his too long hair back from his eyes and jerked his head toward the shed. "Come with me."

Riley accompanied him and waited while he unlocked the door.

"It's a shame the way things have been disappearing around here," Dave commented as the key snicked in the lock. "People been reporting gas gone from their tanks and chickens from their chicken houses. Even been some cars stolen."

Riley swallowed, eaten with guilt over knowing who was stealing at least some of it. "It's a shame what some people will do." He meant it.

"Sure is. Well, here she is." Dave went to a machine propped against the west wall. "Whatcha gonna do with a girl's bike?"

"Not sure."

Dave paused and eyed him studiously. "What's going on?"

Riley hesitated. He had hoped Dave would not ask questions he didn't want to answer. "I found out why she sold it."

Now Dave's interest intensified. "Are you gonna tell me, or is it a secret?"

Riley gripped the handlebars and rolled the bike toward the door. "She sold it so she could buy the school's old piano and give it to her little sister for Christmas."

Dave followed him out and locked the door behind them. "You aim to give it back to her for Christmas?"

Riley stopped and faced Dave. They had been friends for a long time, but he felt exposed at trying to explain motives he hadn't analyzed too closely himself.

"I'm not sure. I just hated to see her give up something she needs. Her car's getting old and probably hasn't had enough maintenance during these past few years. When it gives her trouble, she rides this to school. Without it she'll have to walk when that happens."

Dave nodded in understanding. "And you don't want to see her have a tough time. I…"

A car pulled up to the gas pump, claiming his attention. Thankful, Riley hefted the bicycle over the side of the buckboard. Then he went to the pail beside the pump and took out the wet rag Dave kept there. He washed the windshield of the customer's car while Dave pumped gas into it. Then he took the dry rag from the side of another pail and wiped the glass dry.

"Wish I had you around all the time helping me," Dave said when the car drove away.

Riley headed for the buckboard. Dave followed him.

"I once thought you and Jolene would get married," he said, wiping his hands again. "If I hadn't already been lassoed by Laura, I would have asked Jolene out after you left."

Taken by surprise, Riley looked at Dave with new eyes. "I had no idea you found her...interesting."

Dave's head bobbed. "I saw her a couple of times with Denver Green, but that didn't last long. Guess she figured out he only wanted someone to take care of his kids after his wife died."

The idea of Jolene marrying someone else created a hollow pit in his stomach. "She's a smart girl."

"She's that," Dave agreed, his head bobbing again. "I can't help but wonder if she's been waiting for you all these years. If you're smart, you'll back up and work out whatever went wrong with you two."

"Nah, she's not interested in me anymore." He climbed up onto the wagon seat. "Thanks for holding on to that for me." He jerked his head toward the back of the wagon and flicked the reins against Daisy's backside.

As he drove home, Riley wondered why Jolene had not married. He didn't believe for a minute it was because of him. No, it had been her duty to raise her sister and take care of her dad, and she would not expect a man to take on all that responsibility for her.

The other thing he wondered about was the bicycle. Now that he had it, how could he return it? Jolene had invited his parents to Christmas dinner. He had planned to stay home, but then she had asked his dad if the menfolk would go get Irene's piano after dinner. He felt he had no choice but to help them with that.

Jolene watched Riley's eyes scan the living room when he entered it behind his parents and youngest sister, Clementine. He hardly seemed to notice the tree she and Irene had decorated with ornaments, most of them handmade. But he spent long moments studying the angels she had hung or attached all around the room.

She followed his gaze to the one on the top of the tree. Then he scanned the ones she had suspended from the ceiling by strings, and the ones she had drawn on heavy paper, cut out with scissors and attached to the curtains and doors. She had them everywhere.

Laughter erupted from Georgia's bedroom where her children and Callie's had been sent to play. A fire popped and crackled in the fireplace. The cozy scene brightened further for her when Riley finished his inspection. His eyes met hers in a look much like he used to do before things got complicated.

Callie's twins came scampering down the hallway, chanting, "Unkie, Unkie," and latched on to his legs.

Riley inched his way to the couch and sank down beside Trace, but the little boys stayed with him rather than divert to their daddy. The picture they formed made Jolene's heart ache. *Lord, I've tried to erase my feelings for him—and failed.*

Lily charged into the room and crawled up next to Riley. "Unkie Wiley, I got a new dolly. Nolie did, too," she added as Georgia's youngest crawled up beside her.

Once again Jolene found amusement at seeing Riley so bombarded with small children that he couldn't figure out what to do with them.

"What did you get, Unkie Wiley?"

He grinned down at Lily and worked a hand around a twin to delve into his coat pocket. He pulled out a new pair of gloves. "I got these to keep my hands warm, and some new socks to keep my feet warm."

Jolene stared. They could have had babies the ages of these. She spun on her heel and escaped to the kitchen.

The smells of bread and roasted turkey filled the room. Dessie had joined Georgia, Callie and Irene. The women bustled about getting everything on the table. Pumpkin pies lined the counter.

"I'll tell everyone it's ready," Irene said.

The house was full to bursting, but Jolene loved it—as did everyone else, judging by the lively conversation and hearty eating. When dessert was served, the men ate quickly.

"I need to take care of some things outside," her dad announced when he finished his pie.

"We'll tag along." Arlie Blake got up and followed him, as did Trace and Riley. Jolene's heart rejoiced at seeing her dad getting around with only a limp and no crutches. Trace, although pale, had come today. Callie said he had insisted he felt up to it, pointing out that eating and having fun would put no strain on him.

The women began the cleanup of both the kitchen and the messy children. No one said anything when the sound of a motor starting in front of the house reached them. Except Irene.

"Where are they going?" she asked, going to the window to peer out.

"We got a sick calf. Arlie probably said he wanted to

run home and check on it. Naturally, they all had to go along. Poor calf."

Dessie's explanation seemed to satisfy Irene. She let the curtains fall back into place and tackled the dishwashing.

An hour later they gathered in the living room and bundled the restless children into their coats so they could take them outside to play. Dessie stayed inside.

They were romping in the snow when Trace's truck pulled into the drive and backed up to the edge of the yard. Arlie, Riley and Sam rode standing up in the back, positioned around an upright piano to keep it steady in its ropes.

Irene, who had been around the side of the house with Lily and Nola, rounded the corner and stopped in her tracks. She stared at the truck in disbelief for several moments. Then she ran to Jolene and grabbed her hands.

"What are they doing with that piano?" she nearly screamed. "Where did it come from? Where is it going?"

Jolene wrapped her arms around her little sister. "Merry Christmas, Irene. That's your gift from me."

She pulled back to stare into Jolene's face. Tears streamed from her eyes. "You can't mean that. You already made me a scarf."

Jolene nodded, blinking back tears of her own at the joy she read on Irene's face. "I mean it."

Irene looked over at the truck, and then back at Jolene, as if unsure whether to run to it or stay with the women.

Jolene made the decision for her. "Let them get it inside. Then we can sing Christmas carols."

"How did you get it?" Irene asked, her feet pumping up and down.

Jolene hugged her again. "It's Christmas. You're not

allowed to ask things like that at Christmas. You just accept your gifts and enjoy them."

Irene's expression sobered, and she brushed her gloved hands across her cheeks. "Thank you, thank you. I'll never get another present as wonderful as this."

It took time and maneuvering for the men to get the instrument across the yard, up the steps, into the house and positioned against the inside wall of the living room.

"Now play us a tune." Arlie wore a big grin as he gave Irene the order. She was happy to comply. First she played "Away In A Manger" for the children to sing. Then she played "Silent Night."

While they sang, Jolene had slipped around the room to give Arlie, Trace and her dad each a hug and whisper her thanks to them for hauling the heavy piano around for her. She had just reached Riley's side when Irene began to play "Hark! The Herald Angels Sing."

He gave her a meaningful look and a little wink. "Do I get one of those hugs?"

"Of course you do." She tried to sound casual, but her heart thumped as her eyes met his deep-set black ones. The rest of the room faded away. She stepped closer and let him put his arms around her waist and pull her to him. She looked up, knowing her face had to be flushed. "Thank you for helping me surprise Irene."

She went up on her toes and brushed a quick, feathery kiss on his cheek. Then she pulled out of his embrace.

A nervous little laugh escaped her as she suddenly remembered the room full of people. Thankfully, she held her feet to the floor long enough to carry her to a chair.

As she listened to the singing, Jolene's heart sang for joy. She loved this time with family and friends, and especially loved that Riley was among them. The glances he sent her way every few minutes made her heart flutter. A vision grew in her mind of doing this every year.

Lord, don't let me dream this way if it's impossible. Riley's special to me. Please draw him to You.

Pale streaks of light began to appear in the east as Riley lugged two full milk buckets to the house. He didn't know how to get Jolene's bike back to her. He had thought to slip it back into its customary place in the Delaneys' shed yesterday, but there had been no opportunity. Then it had occurred to him that Irene didn't even know the bicycle was missing. So he sure couldn't ask her to help him.

No nearer a conclusion than ever, he left the milk for Clem to strain and went to work at the mill with his dad. They were making good time when Riley glanced up and saw a big black horse with a white diamond on its long nose coming across the field. Sam Delaney sat in the saddle, the noise of the saw having kept them from hearing him until he was nearly upon them.

Riley tossed a board onto the growing pile and gave his dad a signal that he was quitting. Arlie read his message and then spotted their visitor. He turned off the motor and went to meet Sam as he dismounted.

"Welcome, neighbor. What brings you out so early?" He stuck out a hand.

Sam shook and released it. "I've come to work. My leg's fine now, and I mean to help you. I know Riley lost a lot of time doing my work."

Riley approached and shook Sam's hand. "That's not necessary."

"If you aim to build a house in the spring, you need a lot more lumber than what you got here. You need help. Don't turn it down when it's offered." His tone was brisk, but Sam grinned.

Riley shook his head in exasperation. "You drive a hard bargain. You sure you're a hundred percent?"

Sam gave a nonchalant shrug. "I'm close enough. Now where should I leave this nag?"

Arlie jerked a thumb toward the barn. "Turn him in the corral so he can run if he wants."

Their output that day was considerably better than usual. The next day Sam showed up again and went with them to skid logs. He was good help—and continued to come each day after getting his own chores done.

The door slammed. Jolene looked up from the lesson plans she was preparing for the return to school the next week. Without stopping to remove her coat and boots, Irene came storming across the room and dropped to the floor before Jolene's chair. Tears trekking down her face, she reached up and put her arms around Jolene's waist. Sobs shook her.

Heart pounding, Jolene put the papers aside and hugged her sister. "What's wrong, baby? Did you hurt yourself?"

Irene shook her head and buried her face in Jolene's lap. "You...you shouldn't...have done it," she blubbered almost incoherently.

Confused, Jolene placed a hand under her chin and pulled her face up. "What shouldn't I have done? Tell me so I can make it right."

"You can't." Irene put a hand over her mouth and cried in earnest. "You s-sold it...so...you...could..."

Understanding filtered through Jolene's brain. "I didn't mean to upset you. I just wanted you to have a piano more than I wanted an old bicycle. It gives me, and everyone, such pleasure to hear you play."

Irene used both hands to wipe her eyes. "But—but you

need your bi…bicycle. When you have c-c-car trouble, you r-r-ride it to—to school."

Jolene couldn't dispute that. "So I'll pray that God will keep the car going. Or I'll walk. It's only a mile to school."

Irene drew a deep breath and regained a little of her composure. "If you have car trouble, you can ride my bike."

Jolene shook her head. "No, baby. You ride two miles to school every day. Don't worry. I'll be fine. You just enjoy your piano and entertain us all."

Irene blinked and tried to smile. "You're so good to me. Someday I'll take care of you. Just you wait and see."

Jolene was still thinking about those warm moments with her sister the next morning when her dad came in with the milk.

"What are your plans for today?" he asked.

She set a platter of eggs on the table next to the bacon Irene had just placed there. "I need to run to town and get a few groceries. Why?"

He shrugged. "Diamond has a sore foot. I was just wondering if you need the car. I can walk to the Blakes' if you do."

"I can take you and come back for you this evening."

"You don't mind?"

"Of course not. It's too cold for you to walk, and I need to get out of the house. I've been inside way more than usual, and I'm getting restless. I might even stop in and see Georgia and her family. They won't be back from her sister's until Monday night, and I miss them."

"You go on and leave the cleanup to me," Irene ordered when they finished breakfast.

Jolene didn't argue. She drove her dad to the Blake farm, retraced her route and went on to town. After her errands were complete, she stopped by the Sullivan place for a visit. Later that afternoon she went back to get her dad.

He, Riley and Arlie were all three on their way from the mill to the house when she arrived. She picked up the sack from the seat next to her and got out of the car, glad to have an excuse to see and speak to Riley again.

"Hello, Mr. Blake," she greeted Riley's dad as she met them.

Arlie Blake returned her greeting and kept walking. Her dad gave her a half smile and headed to the car. Riley stopped in front of her.

She extended the sack to him. "Clem's Sunday school class is doing a play at tomorrow night's New Year's Eve service at the church, and she asked to borrow some things for her costume. Will you give this to her?"

He took it. "What's she dressing up to be?"

"I'm not sure. I guess you'll have to attend to find out."

No sooner had the words left her mouth than Jolene regretted them. She had promised herself she would never again press him about going to church.

His eyes dropped closed. His head went back, and his jaw twitched. "I have work to do."

She stepped back, as if she could retreat back over the boundary she had crossed. "I understand." She said it quietly, but wanted to scream. Just like that the camaraderie—or whatever it was—that had existed between them recently was gone.

She turned around and saw that her dad had the car door open. "Coming," she called, hoping neither he nor Arlie had overheard that brief conversation.

Chapter 11

Riley shoved his fists in his pockets and trudged to the house from the barn. He regretted his cold response to Jolene's suggestion that he attend church tonight. He had no idea what they would do at a New Year's Eve service, but it wouldn't have hurt him to go see what his sister—and Jolene—were doing.

God loves you. You can always talk to God about anything.

Sam Delaney's words came back to him. To a man of faith like Sam, they were truth. As for Riley, he had learned at a young age that talking to God led to no visible results or comfort. He did not feel loved by God.

To attend tonight's service after having rebuffed Jolene's hint would only make him patronizing and hypocritical. But something else occurred to him. No one would be home at the Delaney farm that night.

After supper Clem gathered her things, including the

sack Riley had delivered to her from Jolene, and put on her coat. "We'll be late getting home." She aimed the words at Riley as she joined her mom and dad at the door.

"I'm going to try to get some extra sleep tonight," he responded to their backs. *After my errand.*

He wished he had the buckboard, but the family had driven it to church. He put on his coat and gloves and went to the barn where he had hidden Jolene's bicycle in the end stall under a pile of hay.

He couldn't transport a bicycle on the back of a horse, so he pushed it to the road and then got on and rode it to the Delaney farm. He put it in the shed where Jolene and Irene normally stored their machines and headed home on foot.

It wouldn't be found real soon, he reasoned. Tomorrow they would probably stay inside cooking and enjoying the holiday. Then Sunday Irene would ride with the family in the car to church and not use her bike all day. School resumed Monday morning, which was when she would likely notice it—if Jolene didn't go to the shed for something else before that.

Cold and depressed, he plodded along the road. He felt bad that he had not gone to church tonight. He knew how disappointing he was to Jolene—and his parents. But going would have been for the wrong reasons, because of pressure rather than a true desire to be there.

Later, in bed, he decided that he truly did want to attend the next church service. Even though his motive was unclear.

They didn't work Saturday. His dad declared that New Year's Day was a time to relax and prepare for a return to hard duty on Monday.

Sunday morning Riley waited until his parents were gone before he saddled Baldy and rode to the church.

Not sure why he didn't want to be seen, he waited at a distance from the building until he was sure the service had started. Then he left the gelding hitched to a sapling and walked around behind the building. He slipped into the rear door and explored the small rooms back there until he found one with a vent through which he would hear the singing.

"In Romans 5:8 we read these words," the preacher announced when the song ended. "'But God commendeth his love toward us, in that, while we were yet sinners, Christ died for us.'"

There was a pause. Then he continued. "In Romans 6:23 we read about God's gift to us. 'For the wages of sin is death, but the gift of God is eternal life through Jesus Christ our Lord.'"

As Riley listened to the man speak about how every person should ask forgiveness for his or her sins and invite the Lord to come into his life, he felt an odd tugging in the region of his heart. Had his attitude been too harsh all these years?

He cringed when sounds of a car horn and whooping and hollering nearly drowned out the preacher's words. He had no doubt who was out there. Disgust filled him.

No longer able to absorb the sermon, he slipped out the back door and headed back to his horse. As he rode home, questions tumbled through his mind.

Jolene shivered as she scraped a fresh inch of snow from the windshield of the car Monday morning. Her dad opened the door and got behind the wheel. The motor sputtered and died. It happened again. Then it started. He got out.

"Let it run and warm up a bit before you take off."

Thankful that no kettles of hot water had been required to get it going, she took his place behind the wheel. "Thanks for looking after me, Dad." She shot a grin at him before he turned and headed for the barn. She was capable of starting the car herself, but she wouldn't complain about him looking after her. It felt too good to have him back on his feet to complain about anything. She pressed the horn to signal for Kurt and Karen to come out and get in the car.

As she started to put the car in motion, she saw Irene come from the shed, pushing her bicycle. Her face beamed as she stopped alongside the car. Jolene rolled the window down to see what she wanted.

"I'm so glad you got it back." Her voice bubbled with happiness.

Jolene frowned in puzzlement. "Got what back?"

Irene's brow furrowed. "Your bicycle. You didn't tell me you just took out a loan against it, or whatever you did."

Jolene didn't know what to think. "Are you saying it's there? In the shed?"

Now it was Irene's turn to be puzzled. "Yes. Didn't you put it there?"

Her head shaking, Jolene stared over at the shed. "You wouldn't joke with me about a thing like that, would you?"

"No, it's there," Irene insisted. "Go look for yourself."

Jolene looked back at the children. "Don't move. I'll be right back."

She literally jumped out of the car and ran to the shed. Sure enough, there sat her bicycle. She checked for the small dent in the right fender and the crack in the side of the leather seat that told her this was no replacement, but the bicycle she had owned for the past eight years.

She returned to the car and aimed an accusing stare at her little sister.

"What did you do, rob a bank to buy that back for me?" No other explanation occurred to her at the moment.

Eyes round with innocence, Irene raised her gloved palms in the air. "I don't know how it got there. I promise."

Jolene opened the car door and looked back at the children. "Do either of you know how that other bicycle got in the shed?"

"No, Miss Delaney. We've been gone all week." Kurt spoke earnestly, as if afraid they were in trouble.

"We just came back last night in time to go to church with you," Karen added. "We don't know anything about your bicycle, Miss Delaney."

"It's okay. I just don't know what to think. I didn't mean to make you feel like you're in trouble. Okay?"

They both nodded.

Jolene turned back to Irene. "Well, we have to get to school. I'll ask Dad about it when I get home this afternoon."

Irene got on her bike and took off. Jolene drove in the opposite direction. She missed having Irene ride to school with her every day. But she seemed happy enough as a freshman in the town high school.

All day the question hovered in the back of Jolene's mind. How could her bicycle have returned? By the time she dismissed the students, a crazy suspicion had formed. She had to find out.

After Daniel finished his janitor duties, Karen and Kurt having volunteered to help him by washing the blackboard, Jolene and the kids went home. She deposited her belongings on the kitchen table. "I need to talk to Dad," she explained to Georgia as she headed back outside.

Georgia looked up from stirring fried potatoes in a skillet. "He's probably in the barn."

Jolene found him milking the cow they called Buttermilk. "Dad, did you buy my bicycle back from Dave?"

He turned on the stool enough to see her over his shoulder. "Not guilty," he said without hesitation. "Irene told me when she got home that it's back. Got yourself a mystery, huh?"

Her mouth set in a firm line, Jolene returned to the car and drove to town. She went directly to the gas station and parked at the curb next to the garage.

She had to wait while Dave finished waiting on a customer, but as soon as the truck drove away she marched up to him and pointed a finger at him. "Tell me what you did with that bicycle you bought from me."

He worked his mouth around in a funny little twist and took his time wiping his hands. "I sold it," he said at last.

She waggled the finger. "Who bought it?"

He tipped his head and smirked.

"It's not funny," she snapped. "Was it Riley Blake?"

"I'm not supposed to tell."

She watched him roll his eyes and bite his lip. She lowered her hand. "Okay, so you can't tell me. Can you tell me it was *not* him?"

He pursed his lips and considered. "Nope."

"Thanks." She whipped around and headed back to her car, her mind in a whirl. She had to see Riley, but it was getting dark. He would be out doing chores. Then they would eat supper and probably go to bed early.

Which reminded her that Georgia and Irene were fixing supper and probably wondering why she wasn't there.

As much as she wanted to go on to the Blake home, she pulled in at her own house.

The next day Jolene went about her teaching routine, but had trouble keeping her mind on the lessons. At the end of the day, she turned from seeing students out the door and spoke to Karen. "Can you and Kurt entertain yourselves while Daniel does his work? I need to go across the road and speak to someone."

"Riley lives over there," said Kurt. He flashed her a grin that was altogether too knowing for an eight-year-old.

She answered it with a stern teacher look. "I'll be back in a few minutes."

The sound of the big saw at the mill carried across the road, so Jolene knew where to look. She trekked across the field and stopped several yards from where Riley and his dad were working. When he looked up, she crooked a finger and beckoned while mouthing the words, "I need to talk to you."

He turned and spoke to his dad. When Arlie turned off the saw, the sudden quiet was almost startling. Arlie grabbed the board they had just sawed and went to the lumber pile with it. Jolene fought the tightness in her chest as Riley came toward her.

"What's wrong?" he asked when he reached her. His breath came out in white puffs of air. He wore that expressionless face that always kept her from knowing what he was thinking.

She wrapped her arms around her waist and raised her eyes to meet his. "I know you brought my bicycle back to me. Why did you do it?"

He looked down at her for a long time, his slitted eyes roaming her face. Finally, he sighed, as if recognizing the futility of denying it. "I wanted to help you—and I could. You need it for emergencies."

Her eyes swam with tears. "You can't afford to do such a thing."

A gust of wind whipped at them. As she tugged her coat collar tighter around her throat, he reached forward and gripped her shoulders. The action brought him a fraction closer to her, along with his outdoorsy scent. "You work hard and need every penny you make. You couldn't afford to give your sister something that would benefit her for many years, so you did a beautiful thing in selling something of yours to buy it."

"I'll pay you back."

He shook his head. "You don't return gifts."

You just accept your gifts and enjoy them.

The words she had spoken to Irene came back to smack her.

Jolene lifted her hands and cupped his face in her palms. Then she went up on tiptoe and brushed a kiss over his cheek. "Thank you."

Then, before she realized what was happening, he pulled her to him and kissed her soundly. He tasted warm and sweet, woodsy and absolutely wonderful. Her world tilted, spun and shimmered. The breath froze in her lungs.

He pulled back suddenly, as if shocked at what he had done. She stepped back, as well. "Thank you," she repeated inanely.

Already handsome, the smile that curved his mouth made him even more so. "You're welcome."

She turned to leave.

"Jolene."

She stopped and looked back.

"Enjoy the bicycle." He touched the brim of his hat and strode back to the mill.

Her feet seemed to skim the ground, like runners over the snow-covered earth. A new lightness filled her as she returned to the school and told Kurt and Karen to get in the car.

Right or wrong, Riley had become an important part of her life again. He was doing too much for her, but his motives felt right. The vision of a future for them grew in her mind.

Lord, don't let me be in love with Riley if it will only lead to a broken heart again. Please touch his heart. Make everything right.

Riley returned to work, emotions coursing through him like a freight train. "It was only a kiss," he muttered under his breath, suddenly afraid.

He should stay away from Jolene Delaney, for her good as well as his own. Even if she were to love him like he feared he loved her, he had nothing to offer her. He had a couple hundred dollars squirreled away and a dream of having his own place, but that's all it was, a dream.

He knew couples who got married and lived with their parents, but there was no way he could bring a wife, and possibly children, into the tiny home of his parents, even if they rebuilt. And he sure couldn't ask a woman to take him to live with her family.

He shouldn't even be thinking about such things. What he should do was join the military and leave here for good—as soon as he and his dad got enough lumber cut.

He found himself thankful for the noise of the saw as his dad returned and they resumed work. It kept them from talking and possibly bringing up subjects, and questions, that his dad's occasional glances said he wanted to ask.

When they quit for the day, Riley spoke before his

dad could. "I'll split some more wood. You go on and do whatever you need to do." He made his escape.

Over the next days he kept his attention focused on work and ignored questioning looks. When he entered the kitchen Saturday evening, the smells of fried meat and onions made his stomach growl. He hadn't realized he was so hungry.

Clem was wound up that night, excited because her sweetheart was supposed to be home in a few weeks. She monopolized the conversation, which was fine with him.

She put her elbows on the table and gazed across it at him. "I saw Jolene come over after school the other day and talk to you." Her smirk indicated she had seen more than just talk.

He felt the color rise up his neck. "It's a free country."

"That's right. You're free to marry that girl, so why not do it? You've liked her forever."

He started to tell her to mind her own business, but the sound of a car pulling up in front of the house interrupted them. He got up from the table and looked out the window. His stomach sinking, he turned back to face the family. "It's the marshal."

He went to the door and stepped outside, suspecting that the man had come to see him. "Hello, Marshal." He extended a hand, and they shook briefly.

"Hello, Riley." Crinkles appeared at the corners of Leon's eyes. "I need your help. Callie's car has been stolen."

Chapter 12

Riley's breath caught. "When?"

"This afternoon. She went to a wedding shower in the south part of town. There were a lot of cars, so she had to park a ways down the street. When she came out to go home, her car was gone. A friend took her straight to the dealership to tell Trace. He called me."

Anger made it hard to speak. "Trace gave her that car when he asked her to marry him. It means more to her than just any car."

Leon nodded his head in understanding. "We've searched the town and everywhere we can think of, but we can't find it. If we don't locate it fast it'll be gone. I have nothing but instinct guiding me, but I think your shifty neighbors took it."

"And you want me to try to get information from them," Riley finished for him, sick to his stomach.

"I'd appreciate some help. Can you get close to them?

Do whatever you can to find out where they hide the cars they steal before taking them to their buyers."

Riley had determined to stay away from those two. Now he was being asked—again—to seek them out. He didn't want to do it, but if there was a chance of recovering his sister's car, he had to do whatever he could to help. He exhaled a long, slow breath. "I'll see what I can do."

"Thanks. If you find out anything, let me know. I don't care what time of day or night it is." Leon touched his hat brim and left.

Riley stood there a moment, pondering what to do, but the penetrating cold chased him inside. He took his coat from a hook on the wall and shoved his arms into it.

"You have to go out?"

His mother's question, coupled with the anxious look on her face, told him she was worried he was in trouble. He wanted to reassure her, but he didn't know how much to tell her.

"Callie's car has been stolen. The marshal wants me to help him look for it."

She placed a hand on his arm and peered up at his face. "Promise me you won't do anything reckless."

"I'm not in any danger, Mom. I'll be careful."

While he caught and saddled Baldy he debated where to look for Troy and Chuckie. Being Saturday night, they most likely would be hanging around town somewhere. He would just have to do the same and hope to run into them.

Once he got to town, he rode up the street, keeping a close eye out for them. He pulled up at the gas station and hitched Baldy to the garage door in plain view.

Dave grinned as he came out of the station and saw him. He pushed his baseball cap back on his head and gave Riley a long, assessing look. "How are things going, my friend?"

"Okay, I guess. Thought I'd get away from the farm for a bit. Okay if I keep you company a little while?" Riley glanced at a car that rolled up the street past them. It was not the Lonigans.

"Sure, come on inside where it's warmer. We can visit and have a soda pop."

Riley followed Dave inside. Tension pulled at him as he dragged one of the two chairs in the place over in front of the plate-glass window where he could see the street—and be seen. He accepted the grape soda Dave brought him.

"I guess you know your gal came in here asking who I sold her bicycle to." Dave perched sideways on the rickety desk, one foot dangling over the side of it.

"Yeah."

"That all you got to say? Did she thank you for it properly?"

"Yeah." Riley grinned.

Dave shook his head in exasperation. "You're as talkative as ever." He looked out at the pump. "There's hardly any business. I ought to go on home, but a customer or two might come in. So I hang around."

"Every little bit helps."

Thankful his friend had dropped the subject of Jolene, Riley relaxed a bit. They chatted about the weather and unimportant matters for a few minutes. Then he spotted the Lonigan car going by. Attempting nonchalance, he downed the last of his soda, put the bottle down and got up. "I guess I'll get out of your way. It was nice chatting with you."

Dave followed him outside. "Come by more often.

I'll let you wash windshields," he said as Riley swung up into the saddle.

"Will do." He rode to the edge of the street and turned toward home. It wasn't the way Troy had driven, but Riley was confident they would make another pass soon. He was right. Before he got halfway down the street they rolled along beside him and slowed to match Baldy's pace.

"Whatcha doing?" Chuckie leaned out the window to ask.

"Going home."

"We're gonna do some target shooting in the morning. You wanta come?"

Thank you, Chuckie, for making it easy.

"Where?" He knew in his gut exactly where it would be.

"That open field next to the church."

He swallowed his disgust. "Okay. I'll meet you there."

Troy gunned the motor, and the car leaped forward with a sputter and a backfire that made Baldy rear and dance sideways. Chuckie leaned farther out the window and roared with laughter.

Riley gritted his teeth and patted the horse's neck. "Whoa, boy."

As soon as the horse settled down, they made a beeline for home. Riley didn't sleep much that night. Up before the first streaks of daylight, he lit a lantern, got the milk buckets and went to the barn.

"You plan to tell me what's going on?"

Absorbed in his thoughts, Riley hadn't heard his dad enter. He got up with the full milk pail and faced him. His troubled expression cut at Riley. His dad deserved the truth.

"Leon asked me to do something that might help get Callie's car back."

Arlie eyed him steadily in the dim glow of the lantern. "I'm afraid that means the Lonigans are involved. I won't ask for details. But will you please be careful?"

His parents had lost one son—and nearly lost Riley five years ago. He understood their fears. "I'll be careful," he promised.

"I'll be praying." His dad reached over and took the milk bucket from him.

Riley went to saddle Baldy. As he rode away, his dad's words rang in his ears. He found them comforting.

Rather than go straight to the field where they were to meet, Riley rode past the church and turned onto a road that wasn't much more than a path. He circled through the woods and searched the area around the Lonigan farm, hoping to spot Callie's car. He hitched Baldy and walked to their barn. There was no sign of life around the place yet, so he looked inside—and found nothing.

Seeing no other buildings big enough to hide a car, he went back to his horse. He widened his circle through the woods, but his search was fruitless. Finally, he gave up and went back to the field where they were to meet.

Riley fought the fresh anger that hit him as Troy and Chuckie drove up and got out. They both looked like they had done some heavy drinking last night.

Chuckie stumbled around the car and took a paper sack from the backseat. "Got us some targets here," he practically shouted, waving the sack in the air.

"Go set 'em up," Troy ordered.

"All right, all right, I'm going. Can't you see," Chuckie groused.

Troy reached inside the car and gave the horn a couple

of punches. He aimed a lopsided grin at Riley as he closed the door and stumbled around in front of it.

Riley slid to the ground and led Baldy a few feet away. Across the field he saw a car pull in at the church, and cringed. He knew someone was bound to recognize him, and envisioned the look of disappointment he would get if that someone happened to be Jolene.

Not only did Riley hate being part of this crazy setup, but he didn't feel safe, either. Troy and Chuckie weren't great shots under the best of circumstances and handled their guns recklessly. Still under the influence of alcohol, they would be downright dangerous.

Troy waved a pistol in front of him. Then he closed one eye and peered unsteadily through the sights. He fired, and the gun jerked his hand back. He grabbed the wrist with his other hand and fired again. Both shots went wild.

Chuckie let out a whoop and fired similar shots, also hitting nothing. They were scary.

Riley decided he had to hurry this along. They were dull witted enough that he couldn't think of a subtle way to get information out of them. So he opted for outright bluntness.

He aimed his own pistol and pulled the trigger. A bottle burst into pieces from the fence post where it had sat. "My sister's car was stolen yesterday."

Suddenly, there was quiet.

"That's too bad." Troy's bleary eyes roamed over him. "Any idea who took it?"

Riley judged Troy was doing a fair job of feigning innocence. He sighted up his gun and faced the targets. "The marshal thinks you guys have it. So don't be surprised if you see him prowling around your place."

He glanced sideways and saw Chuckie shoot a furtive

look at his older brother. Troy was the one he needed to scare into checking on their hidden goods. Chuckie was already so scared he was about to explode.

"Dad'll run him off," Chuckie declared. "He might even shoot him."

"Aw, shut up," Troy snapped. "He won't do no such stupid thing as shoot a lawman. Besides, he don't need to. The man ain't gonna find no stolen car around our place."

Not there.

Riley fired, and hit another bottle.

As the noise outside escalated, Pastor Denlow stepped to the pulpit. He waited until the congregation ended their song. "Ladies and gentlemen, we have a problem. Something has to be done about this continued disturbance. We can't act in an unchristian manner because others are disrespectful of God's house and our worship time. But God can handle it."

"Amen," came from several people.

"Let's all kneel right where we are and seek God's help."

As the pastor knelt by the pulpit, Jolene turned and got on her knees before her pew. Her dad and Irene knelt beside her. All around the room other members did the same.

"Lord, we beseech You to intercede in order that we may worship You in peace," the pastor prayed. When he finished, someone else prayed. Then another.

Suddenly, the noise stopped.

Jolene opened her eyes and looked around. Others were doing the same thing. Smiles broke out on their faces, and people got to their feet.

Thank You, Lord.

"Please continue the song service," the pastor said.

Then he went to the door and disappeared outside. As they finished a song, he returned, his face aglow.

"It's raining in that field," he announced. "And nowhere else."

Riley lowered his gun and glanced up at the rain that had burst from the sky. Several small clouds floated together and formed a picture that made him gasp. It looked like one of Jolene's snow angels.

"Let's get out of here before that stuff freezes," Chuckie shouted as the sky darkened and the rain became a downpour.

Riley hesitated as the brothers ran to the car. He didn't want to go with them. But he wanted to know where they were going. His gut said they would not go home. He ran to Baldy and swung into the saddle.

When the car sped away, he nudged Baldy and followed it. To his surprise, they ran out of the rain within seconds. He twisted around in the saddle and saw dark clouds still hovering over the field. A shiver ran up his spine.

He looked back at the road just in time to see the car slow to a snail's pace, as if Troy had also been startled by the unexpected weather phenomenon and was uncertain whether to keep on toward home, or go somewhere else.

Riley slowed Baldy to a walk and fell farther behind. Moments later the car picked up speed again. He did the same—and his heartbeat quickened when it swung left at the fork in the road rather than going on toward home.

Knowing he was about to lose them, he steered Baldy across the ditch and into the woods. They worked through the trees and caught up with the car on the other side of the hill. In a burst of insight he knew where they were headed.

Houses stood abandoned around the countryside where families had been evicted after foreclosures. No one could afford to buy them, so they sat there boarded up and going to ruin. The farm Georgia Sullivan and her husband had lost was one of those homes, and it was located at the end of that lane.

Riley wanted to follow them on to the house, but he couldn't afford to waste the time. He whirled Baldy around and headed for town, pushing the horse as hard as he could without risking harm to him. He circled around the edge of town and took every shortcut he could think of to Leon's house. At the gate he slid to the ground and ran to the door. He banged on it. No one answered.

Kicking himself for coming after the marshal instead of confronting Troy and Chuckie, he headed back to the gate. He swung back into the saddle and turned the horse around. And stopped at the sight of Leon driving up the street with his wife and kids in the car. Their clothes said they had been to church. He pulled in next to Riley and got out.

"You got something?"

Riley nodded and stayed mounted. "I followed Troy and Chuckie to the abandoned Sullivan farm. I didn't go on up the lane, but my guess is that's where they're hiding the stolen cars, probably in the barn."

"Thanks. I'll take care of it. Go on home and stay out of sight."

Riley opened his mouth to argue.

"I said go home," the marshal repeated, cutting him off. "I don't want you involved."

Riley didn't like it, but he got it. Leon had his information and was doing him the favor of keeping Troy and Chuckie from knowing for sure who had fingered them.

* * *

"Brr, it's too cold to be outdoors." Juanita Tomlin swept through the doorway Jolene had opened at her knock. "I baked bread this afternoon so the extra heat would help warm the house. I thought I would share it with my neighbors. I know how much Sam loves fresh bread."

Jolene stifled a spurt of amusement and accepted the neighborly offering. The woman undoubtedly had "news" she wanted to share, and the bread provided an excuse to visit.

"Thank you, Mrs. Tomlin. I'm sure he'll love it." *But not your gossipy purpose behind the visit.* They all knew to be careful not to say anything in the woman's presence that they didn't want everyone in the community to know.

"I don't have but a minute. I need to get back home."

Jolene took the bread to the kitchen table and came right back. "It's too bad you don't have time to sit and visit."

"Have you heard that the marshal arrested Troy and Chuckie Lonigan this afternoon?"

The news took her aback. "What were they arrested for?" *Disturbing the peace?*

"Callie Gentry's car was stolen yesterday. He caught them red-handed with it. I hear they had it hidden over in the deserted Sullivan farm."

Jolene stared at the woman's smug expression. "No, I hadn't heard." She had not been to visit Callie that weekend, and Callie had left church immediately after service to have dinner with her husband's parents. There had been no time to visit.

"Well, I knew you'd be interested since she's such a good friend of yours. But I declare, I don't know what to think of that brother of hers."

"You mean Riley?"

"That's exactly who I mean. I recognized him out in that field next to the church with those two this morning." She shook her head in disdain. "I don't know if he's involved in their stealing, but he's bound to get in trouble—if he's not already—if he's hanging around with them."

Jolene's stomach plummeted, and her breath came in short, quick gasps. She couldn't bear to hear any more.

"Thank you for the bread. It was thoughtful of you."

Juanita pulled her coat tighter around her and headed for the door.

Jolene hurried to open it, lest the woman change her mind and stay longer. Thankfully, she went on out and walked to her car.

Chapter 13

Jolene sank onto the sofa and closed her hand over the arm of it in a white-knuckled grip. Sick of heart, she ached with pangs of despair. She wanted to scream, or weep, and could do neither.

How could he? He said it wouldn't happen again.

Lord, please let Juanita be mistaken.

Irene came back into the room. "I'm sorry to leave you like that, but I…" She stopped and took a closer look at Jolene. "You're upset. What did that old chigger say to you?"

Jolene moved her head back and forth. "Callie's car was stolen yesterday, but they got it back. The Lonigans have been arrested for stealing it."

"Then you should be happy. That means they won't be hanging around the church and disrupting services."

"Maybe."

"So what's wrong?"

"She also said that Riley was with them this morning."

"Oh." Irene stood there a moment, and then flung herself down beside Jolene. She hugged her. "Georgia and the kids won't be back for another hour or two. Dad's outside doing chores. Why don't you go lie down for a while? The peace and quiet will be good for you."

Listless and heartsick, Jolene took her little sister's advice. But all she could do was lie there awake, unable to escape the constant thoughts and questions.

Why, Lord? Why would he risk hanging around with them and getting into trouble?

She wept. When she was empty, she sat up and ran a hand through her messy hair and rubbed her puffy eyes. "You let yourself start dreaming again," she scolded herself. "You knew better. You're destined to stay single. Accept it and be content."

Help me do it, Lord.

She went to the kitchen and helped Irene prepare a light evening meal.

The next day Jolene pushed her misery to the back of her mind and got ready for school. She had responsibilities to meet. Her students needed to learn. And her dad and sister counted on her to keep their home functioning.

As the day passed, anger festered. Riley would never hurt her again. She wouldn't let him. She refused to look across the road where he lived and worked, even when she monitored the children outside during recess. She didn't want to see him.

She knew that Riley had known hunger as a boy, and his family had suffered the loss of his older brother. Even though only a year older than she was, his perspective had been different, especially about money. He had gotten involved in bootlegging with the Lonigans for the money his family needed, rather than a desire to be dishonest or live a wild life. His mistake had been in trying to solve his problems on his own and not ask God for help—and he had paid a price.

His credibility had been damaged. Being shot by a gangster who mistook him for his sister had nearly cost him his life.

Jolene dismissed the students and went back inside the school to mark papers while Daniel did his janitorial chores. Kurt and Karen washed the blackboard for him again. Absorbed in her work, a noise startled her. She looked up with a jolt to see that Riley had entered the room with Daniel. They each dumped an armload of wood in the box.

Riley's eyes met hers. She tried to read his face. Was that fear she recognized? Or arrogance? The tightness in her chest smothered her. A need to confront him assailed her.

She glanced at the listening ears in the room. When Riley turned and headed out, she got up and snatched her coat from the back of her chair, putting it on as she followed him.

Riley marched to the woodpile to get another armload. He had been on his way to the house from the mill when the sight of Daniel carrying in wood had spurred an impulse to help. In all honesty, it was probably rooted in the hope of seeing Jolene and gauging her reaction to him.

As he picked up a stick of wood, a sound made him pause and turn around. Jolene stood there, her expression forbidding. She gave him a visual inspection that made him freeze inside. Yes, she knew he had been with Troy and Chuckie yesterday morning. No, she was not ready to hear an explanation. They both stood stock-still while Daniel filled his arms and headed back inside the building.

"I heard that you were part of that racket in the field with the Lonigans during church yesterday morning. Were you?"

"Yeah, I was with them." He focused on a distant point beyond her rather than say the thing he was thinking. He could not—would not—deny it, but the less he said, the better.

"You said it wouldn't happen again."

He ground his back teeth together. "I said racing with them wouldn't happen again."

The color drained from her face, and she drew in a short, quick breath. "Why?"

His jaw twitched at the annoyance her expression displayed. She clearly wasn't in a frame of mind to hear the truth. "If you don't believe in me, nothing I could tell you would make any difference. You don't know nearly as much about me as you think you do."

She laughed, a bitter, tortured sound. "You know those two are trouble. They have no respect for God, the church or the people who worship there. How could you be part of their deliberate disruptions?"

"I guess so you can have a reason to preach at me," he returned hotly. "Just like you've always done."

Her eyes closed. Then she raised her head and said in a near shout, "I wanted you to be a Christian because I loved you and wanted to marry you, and the Bible says a Christian should not marry an unbeliever."

As her words left her mouth, she spun on her heel and ran back toward the school.

Already freezing from standing there in the cold, her words hit Riley like a dowsing in frigid water.

He considered following her, but didn't. Nothing he

could do or say would change anything. She may have loved him once. She sure didn't now. Even if she still did, he wasn't good enough for her.

The woodpile forgotten, he shoved his hands in his coat pockets and headed back across the road—where he belonged.

Jolene stumbled back inside the building, her cheeks burning. Why had she spoken to him that way?

Lord, I'm sorry. He might never trust in You now. And it's my fault. Please forgive me. Touch his heart. Do whatever it takes to draw him to You.

"Are you two ready to leave?" she asked Kurt and Karen, struggling to appear composed.

Karen pulled on her gloves. "Daniel left. He said he plans to come extra early in the morning to build the fire since it's so cold."

Jolene nodded, hardly hearing the words. She had to get the kids home before they froze now that the fire had gone out in the stove.

When they arrived at the house, she was surprised to see Callie's car parked in front of it. She loved seeing her friend at any time, but right now she dreaded the possibility of having Riley's name come up in a conversation. She pasted a smile on her face and followed the children inside.

Callie came from the kitchen, a twin in her arms. She put the little one down and met Jolene at the edge of the room to hug her.

"Trace told me something this afternoon," she said without preamble when she backed away. She aimed a probing look into Jolene's eyes. "I wanted to get over here and talk to you before you heard about it. But I didn't make it in time, did I?"

Jolene swallowed and tried to smile, but failed miserably. "It depends what you're talking about."

"Come over here." She pulled Jolene down onto the sofa beside her. Then, as if taking care of one of her children, she unbuttoned her coat, pushed it down her shoulders and tugged the sleeves from her arms. Jolene just sat there and let her.

Callie turned to the children. "Georgia has fresh cookies in the kitchen. Why don't you all go get one?"

She smiled as the Sullivan children scampered away with her own. "Now," she said when they were alone. "You must have heard about my car being stolen and the Lonigans being caught with it. Am I right?"

Jolene nodded mutely.

"And you also heard that Riley was with them yesterday morning?"

She nodded again.

Callie's mouth tightened. "I thought so. Well, the story is true. But there's more to it. No, you sit right there and hear me out," she ordered when Jolene tried to get up. She pressed a hand against her shoulder.

"When Trace came home after work a while ago, he said Leon stopped by the car business for a chat. He shared information that he said can't be common knowledge because the Lonigans might seek revenge against Riley."

Jolene stiffened. Instinct told her to prepare for something unpleasant.

"Leon went to Riley after he couldn't find my car. He thought Troy and Chuckie had taken it, but he didn't know where to find it. He asked Riley to spend time with them some more and try to find out where they hide the stuff they've been stealing. Riley accepted their invitation to target shoot, and then followed them to the abandoned Sullivan farm. Then he rode to town and told Leon."

Jolene blinked as she struggled to comprehend Riley's role in the story. "He couldn't refuse to help Leon when it was his sister's car they had stolen," she reasoned aloud.

Callie's head moved in the affirmative. "He made it possible for me to get my car back."

Jolene knew how much that car meant to Callie. So did Riley. "He did what he had to. He's a hero." The words came out in a strangled whisper as her anger drained away.

"I wanted you to know. Are you all right?" Callie ̖stared at her frozen expression.

Jolene nodded and cleared her throat. "I'm fine. Thank you for coming to tell me."

Callie gave her another hug and got up. "I hate to gossip and run, but I don't have supper even started. Trace will understand, but the kids won't."

Jolene could hardly eat the supper that Georgia put before them minutes after Callie left.

You hurt him.

The thought ate at her. Why did she always hurt Riley? She thought she had changed, grown less judgmental and more tolerant, but she hadn't. No matter how hard it would be to face him, she had to apologize. It was too late to go to his house tonight. She would go after school tomorrow.

After a sleepless night, she spent a difficult day. What she had to do weighed on her through every hour, every duty. As soon as she dismissed the students, she spoke to Kurt and Karen. "I have to run an errand. I'll be right back."

"We'll be fine, Miss Delaney," Kurt assured her.

"We'll help Daniel," Karen added.

Jolene put on her coat and gloves and marched across the road, steeling herself to face Riley. But it wasn't necessary. He was not at the house, and no one knew where he had gone. She suspected he had seen her coming and dodged her.

She tried again the next afternoon. And the next.

She drove home, peering ahead into the lightly falling snow. How could she make things right? Riley clearly had no intention of letting her near him again. She realized she loved him, but had no hope of a life with him.

"Lord, help him understand that he's loved by You— and me. I can't do anything about my feelings for him. They're a part of me. Please put someone in his life who will convince him of Your love."

Riley worked himself senseless, taking care to be far from the house when school dismissed each day. Jolene was bound to learn the truth about his role in recovering Callie's car. Knowing what a stickler she was for doing the right thing, she undoubtedly would feel obligated to apologize to him. But he didn't want a meaningless apology.

While the lumber pile grew, a thousand thoughts hammered at him. In spite of Jolene's distrust of him, he still had feelings for her. Deep down he feared that he loved her. But he knew his place. He was just a poor man with nothing but his two hands and a dream of building a home of his own. He had a history of mistakes and nothing to offer a woman. Jolene was pretty, educated and capable. Even if she truly did love him, his pride would never let him ask her to marry him and end up being supported by her. He would get over this ache that ate a hole in his heart.

He lay awake at night, wearing his clothes and huddled

beneath every quilt and blanket he could find not in use to keep warm. The northwest side of the house where his bed was located caught the worst of the wind and winter elements. The one thing that gave him a measure of satisfaction was that they had enough lumber cut to start building the new house as soon as the weather turned warmer. He tried to keep his focus on that.

The next day Clem came in from checking the mailbox after lunch and extended an envelope toward him. "Here's a letter addressed to you."

He took it and stuffed it inside his coat pocket, reluctant to open it in front of her.

She smirked. "Got a girlfriend we don't know about?"

"No. And it wouldn't be any business of yours if I did." He reached over and tweaked her nose. "Go chase the dog or something." He turned and followed his dad out the door.

Back at the mill, he looked out across the pasture to the school. A blob of snow fell from a big tree near the building and landed with a plop.

Restless and wrestling with whether he should leave, he turned and fastened his attention on the pile of logs they had skidded that morning. He loved this place and hated the thought of leaving again. He wanted to help get the new house built, but he needed to go. Sick at heart, he pulled the letter from his pocket. And gulped when he saw who had written him. He opened it and began to read.

"Whatcha got there, son?"

His dad's question reclaimed his attention. "Clyde Wilcox, my WPA boss, wants me back on his crew."

Creases formed between his dad's brows. "You going?"

Riley drew a deep breath. "I think I should."

Arlie nodded. "Do whatever you need to do. You've

been a big help, and we've got enough lumber to practically build a whole house."

He hated to leave his dad to do the job alone. It was so like him to never complain, but just deal with things as they happened. But Riley knew that Trace and other friends would help. He swallowed the hard knot in his throat.

"I'll pack my suitcase tonight. Clem can ride double with me on Baldy to Callie's and bring the horse home. I'll catch a bus to Springfield."

Chapter 14

"Riley's gone."

Jolene stared at Callie, feeling the blood drain from her face. "Wh...where did he go?"

"He went back to work for the WPA."

Fortunately, Callie had twins clambering on her lap to distract her from how much the news had upset Jolene. She put a coat on one little boy and set him down. While she bundled the second twin, the first one proceeded to take his coat back off.

Welcoming an excuse to occupy herself, Jolene bounced off the sofa and caught the little guy before he could completely undress himself.

That explained why she hadn't seen Riley around the house or mill—not that she had been looking—all week. Had he really needed to go, or had he been so desperate to avoid her that he had grabbed a job just so he could leave?

"Lily cried when he left, and she asks about him all the

time. Trace and I may take the kids to see him next month on his birthday—if the weather doesn't get too bad."

Callie set the little boy on the floor and got up. Then she looked into Jolene's frozen expression and wrapped her in a warm embrace. "Oh, dear. I was afraid you were hurting. That's why I didn't say anything sooner."

Jolene shrugged and pulled back. Her spine stiffened. "I'm fine." She wanted to scream or cry, or both. But she managed to control the impulses.

Callie studied her for a minute, and then took a deep breath. "My brother is a stubborn mule. He's staying with Aunt Lily and working in Springfield when he could be here with you. He's running, you know."

Jolene shook her head. "He's doing what he thinks is best."

Trace stepped inside the door. "Callie, are you and the kids ready to go home?"

"The boys are. I sent Lily to put on her coat." She turned and called toward the hallway. "Lily, it's time to go."

Karen Sullivan appeared, leading Lily by the hand. "She's ready, but she doesn't want to go."

Lily stuck out her lower lip. "I want to play with Nola and Karen some more."

"We need to go. Thank Miss Jolene for having us over for dinner."

Lily turned her luminous eyes onto Jolene. Then she ran to her. "Fank you, Miss Jolene. The chicken was good."

Jolene hugged the little girl and was able to produce a genuine smile. "Good enough to make you cluck?"

Lily giggled. "Yep. Cluck, cluck."

Jolene released her to her mother. "I wish you could

stay longer, but your mom and dad want to get home before the snow and ice that are predicted get here."

Jolene followed them to the door but didn't go out into the frigid air. When they were gone, she told Georgia she needed a Sunday afternoon nap and escaped to her room.

She crawled onto the bed and stared up at the ceiling, heartsick with regret. Riley would never love her now. She had not trusted him. Surely he had not absolutely had to leave so soon. Yes, he had said he was home for the holiday season to be with his parents and help them. Then he had spent a lot of work time here helping her dad. Surely he and Arlie did not have enough lumber for a house yet.

When she heard her dad and Irene enter the house, she didn't stir. Clouds of despair made her hide away like a naughty child avoiding its parents. When clicking sounds on the windows signaled that sleet had begun to fall, she closed her eyes.

Homebound all the past week because the weather and roads were too bad to have school, Jolene pasted on a normal facial expression and listlessly went about performing tasks that should have been simple but seemed to take more energy that she possessed. But she was aware of the questioning looks Georgia, Irene and her dad directed at her. No doubt they suspected—or knew—what ate at her, but they did not press her for conversation.

She tried to read her Bible, but the formerly comforting passages brought no solace now. Nor could she concentrate on her schoolbooks and lessons. She drifted through the days as if she were a sled coasting across the snow with no hands steering it.

When Sunday came around again, she didn't bother to take off her bathrobe and get dressed.

"I don't feel up to going this morning," she told her

dad when he asked when she would be ready to leave for church.

He shook his head slowly. "Life goes on, girl. Please don't stay home and avoid people. You need to be in the services and around friends when you feel bad."

"Not today. Maybe next week." She picked up her plate and took it to the dishpan. She had eaten only a few bites. She couldn't bring herself to sit in the service and pretend that everything was normal when she hurt so badly. She knew God could restore her zest for life, but she simply didn't have the will to worship right now.

Sam sighed in resignation. "I can't make you. And it wouldn't help your depression if I did."

When she was alone in the house, Jolene started to go back to bed. But a nudge of conscience made her stop. Instead, she went to the desk in the section of the big living room that she used for an office and got out a pen and paper. She sat down and began to write a letter to Riley, apologizing and asking forgiveness for her lack of faith in him and for trying to force him into being what she wanted.

When she finished, she folded the paper, put it in an envelope and sealed it. Then she put it in her purse. So far, so good. She felt a tiny bit better.

When Callie drove up that afternoon, as Jolene had anticipated would probably happen, she opened the door.

"Save your breath," she greeted her friend with a wan smile. "I've already scolded myself. I promise I won't hide out and miss church again. I'm ready for school tomorrow. But I do want to ask a favor."

Callie stepped inside and hugged her. "Hallelujah. I knew you would snap out of that depression soon. What can I do for you?"

"First, you can come have a nice cup of hot tea with

me. Then—" she reached into her purse and extracted the letter "—you or Trace can give this to Riley when you go to see him. I don't know where to send it." She held out the letter.

Callie hesitated a moment to study her before taking it. Then she smiled. "We'll see that he gets it."

Gusts of late February ice-flecked rain soaked Riley as he walked to Aunt Lily's house after work, the dampness bone-chilling. The cold seared his lungs and numbed his face. He directed his thoughts to warm memories.

Last summer he had stayed with his aunt when he worked on the gigantic outdoor swimming pool at the Southwest Missouri State University campus. With Aunt Lily having already made it known that she would welcome him to stay with her, as Callie had once done, he had preferred the Springfield assignment over projects closer to home that would have required commuting or staying in a work camp.

The slow-paced excavation work had been done by pick and shovel, and the debris hauled away in wheelbarrows. In his opinion, the cynics who referred to the WPA as meaning, "We Piddle Around," had no idea what backbreaking labor it had been.

After almost eighteen months of continuous employment with the program, the typical maximum length of time WPA workers could work consecutively, he had gone home. His foreman's request for him to return had been propitious.

Life moved on, but at a snail's pace. Confusion and an aching heart dogged him through the work-laden days and sleepless nights. Why couldn't he shake his feelings for Jolene? Why did her "preaching" words and ways creep into his thoughts at every turn?

The pastor's words he had listened to in the back room of the church also nagged at his heart and spirit. Did the loving God they both spoke of care about an Ozark hick like him?

He went over and over everything, trying to make sense of his life. He had never been so confused. "Are you there, God? Do You care what I do? Should I stay here and work? Or go home and look after the folks?"

And Jolene.

He shook off the last.

After supper with Aunt Lily, he took a bath and went to his bedroom. His aunt insisted he not pay her room and board, but send the money to his mother, her sister, instead.

He picked up the Bible that lay on top of the dresser. Then, sitting on the bed, he leafed through it. What book had the preacher been reading from?

Romans.

Yes, that was it. But what chapter? He couldn't remember. His eyes locked on the page that lay open in chapter ten. He began to read.

That if thou shalt confess with thy mouth the Lord Jesus, and shalt believe in thine heart that God hath raised him from the dead, thou shalt be saved. For with the heart man believeth unto righteousness; and with the mouth confession is made unto salvation.

What did that mean?

He read on. His attention particularly caught on verse thirteen. *For whosoever shall call upon the name of the Lord shall be saved.*

This stuff sounded too easy. Could the answer be that simple? What about his fifteen-year-old brother's death? How could this God he was reading about let that happen?

He wished he could talk to the pastor. Or Trace.

* * *

The next day Riley spent his birthday at work as usual. Wanting to get home to the birthday dinner his aunt had told him to expect, he took a shortcut across a vacant lot on his way home from work.

He was about two-thirds of the way across the lot when he came to an abrupt stop. He looked around, but didn't see anything. He started to move forward again, but an inner feeling he didn't understand held him rooted in place. He gazed ahead of him in the near dark. Suddenly, there was a loud crack and a giant limb crashed noisily from the nearby oak tree, landing right in front of him. Then, to Riley's shock, the earth opened up and swallowed it.

He inched forward and peered down into a big black hole. Invisible under the snow, a layer of boards had covered an abandoned well. Old and rotten, they had splintered. If he had stepped onto those rotten boards, he could have been seriously injured—or killed. He could even have lain there all night and frozen to death.

Shaken, he looked around again, and wondered if God had warned him in his spirit. His legs trembled as he walked on to his aunt's house. His close brush with death made him think about heaven and hell and eternity. His arms wrapped around his torso for warmth, he stared up into the dark sky and the twinkling stars. He would have to ponder this when he wasn't so tired and cold.

When he got to the house, he was surprised to find Callie and Trace's car parked at the curb. He had barely stepped inside the living room when three little people charged at him.

"Unkie Wiley, Unkie Wiley." Lily leaped into his arms. Each twin clutched a leg.

"Happy birthday, big brother," Callie greeted him

from the doorway across the room. Trace stood beside her. Aunt Lily came from the kitchen, a smug smile on her face.

"Supper is ready," she announced.

"Did you know they were coming?" Riley asked as he released the children and took his place at the table.

She dipped her head. "Yep. It was a hard secret to keep."

She had prepared his favorite foods, so Callie had to have conspired with her. The best thing, though, was having loving family around him.

After birthday cake and the presentation of a new pair of overalls, he thanked everyone, got up and gave Trace a pointed look. "You got time to talk? I'd like to ask you about something."

"Sure." Trace studied him, seeming to sense the seriousness of his mood. "Want to go to your room?"

Riley nodded, thankful that his brother-in-law sensed his desire for privacy. He led the way to his room. "Have a seat." He pointed at the only chair and sat on the side of the bed. Then he faced Trace head-on.

"Since I was eight I've blamed God for my brother's death. It didn't seem that He cared about me, so why should I care about Him?"

Trace nodded. "I went through that when my fiancée died. I was a Christian, but I withdrew from God. I had to learn that he still cared about me and that he had another plan for my life than what I had thought."

Riley listened—really listened. Trace was a good man, a dear friend who cared about him. He could trust him.

Riley rocked back and forth. "God has been showing me some things, making me think about eternity. What should I do?"

Trace drew a deep breath. "You just open up your

heart and ask God to forgive your sins and come into your life."

"Like what I read last night," he murmured as he accepted the simplicity of it. Then he bowed his head. "I'm sorry, Lord, for blaming You and turning away from You. Please forgive me and come into my life."

As the sincere words left his mouth, he felt light and clean throughout his body and soul. The hurting and guilt he had carried for so long eased, and moisture filled his eyes. He raised his head and smiled, feeling real joy for the first time in ages.

Trace leaned forward and extended a hand. "Welcome into the kingdom of God, buddy. Now I think you're ready to handle whatever is in this."

Riley released his hand and watched him take a folded envelope from his shirt pocket and hold it out. A letter?

"Jolene Delaney asked us to give this to you."

Riley swallowed and paused before he reached out and took it. God had forgiven him. Could Jolene possibly do so, as well?

Trace stood. "I'll leave so you can read it in private. I'm praying for you." He went to the door but paused and looked back. "She's a good woman, Riley. And I suspect she loves you. Don't let pride keep you from her."

When the door clicked shut behind him, Riley sat there without moving, absorbing Trace's words and working up the courage to open the letter. Then he steeled himself and tore the end off the envelope. He began to read.

Dear Riley,
Please forgive me for the way I spoke to you when I should have been thanking you for helping Leon locate Callie's car and put those thieves out of business. Thank you.

My feelings for you have always made me want and expect too much of you. Yes, I still want you to become a Christian, but no longer from selfish reasons. I tried to force you to be what I wanted, do things my way, and only drove you away. I am so sorry.

I'm praying for God to guide and protect you.

Despite our differences, I want only the best for you and for you to be happy.

Jolene

Riley swallowed a choking sound and raised his eyes. His heart crumbled. Loving that silly woman was killing him. How like her to say she was praying for him even as she apologized for pressuring him.

Blinking, he stared up at the ceiling and swiped the back of a hand over his eyes.

Then, ever so slowly, his mouth tightened in resolve. He had amends to make. Could he do it? Could she love him again?

He had to find out.

Chapter 15

Jolene stood in the root cellar and studied the dwindling supplies. The shelves had once been filled with canned meat, vegetables, jams and jellies, beet and cucumber pickles and canned fruit. Bins had held potatoes, carrots, apples and turnips. Milk, cream and butter still cooled on the concrete floor, but the shelves and bins were nearly depleted. Last year's garden had not been as bountiful as in the past.

As she stood praying about getting this year's garden planted as soon as possible, along with automatic requests for Riley's safety and well-being, a sense of waiting filled her. The days had followed a pattern since his departure. She had concentrated on her work and family and done her best to ignore her loneliness.

"Thank you, Father, for still working in my life. My students and family are doing well. We have the necessities for survival. Please show me daily what you would have me do."

The sound of a car outside interrupted her prayer. She took a jar of tomatoes from the top shelf and headed out into the yard. The chilly air cut through the long sleeves of her blue cotton dress.

Spring, her favorite time of the year, was so close she could smell it. New life emerging all around them always brought a fresh surge of life to her flagging spirits after the cold and trials of winter. With the early March weather clearing, the end of the school year was only weeks away.

Georgia Sullivan and her children emerged from Juanita Tomlin's car. She must have picked them up on their way here. Jolene heard Georgia thank "the chigger" for the ride before coming across the yard. Her appearance had improved during her time here, but the expression on her face had lost its air of peace. There was strong emotion there, but was it excitement or distress? They met at the bottom of the porch steps.

"I got a letter from my husband," Georgia said without preliminaries. "He got a job in Salem."

"That's wonderful," Jolene said with sincere enthusiasm.

Her face did a funny little twist that was half smile, half frown. "He's staying with a cousin, and he wants me and the kids to come join him."

Which was great for her, but brought back the dilemma of the kids and school. Jolene weighed the matter rapidly. "You can leave Kurt and Karen here until the end of school if you want and your husband approves. It's only a little over two months."

Georgia's whole body sagged with relief. Tears wound down her cheeks. "Thank you again, Miss Delaney.

You've been so good to all of us. I hate to take advantage of you, but I know the kids, especially Kurt, would be happier if they could finish the term here. By fall maybe a change of school, in a new community, will be easier."

Jolene set the tomatoes down and opened her arms. Georgia promptly stepped into her embrace. "I'm glad I can help," Jolene said when they parted. She picked up the tomatoes. "Let's go in and make a pot of soup."

Change was definitely in the air.

It felt good to be back in Deer Lick. A riot of emotions threaded through Riley as he emerged from Dave's gas station into the pleasant late-March air. Main Street had very little traffic today.

He had a job. It might not be permanent, but he had a job.

After giving control of his life to the Lord, he had decided he would quit the WPA at the beginning of spring. As he made plans to return and help his dad build the house and ask Jolene to go out with him, a letter had come from Dave Freeman. Dave's wife needed to move to St. Louis to undergo lengthy medical treatment and be near her doctors. Dave had talked to Trace and come up with a plan. Dave would get someone to run the station while he was gone. But if it developed that he had to live in St. Louis permanently, they would work out a deal for Trace to buy the station. They wanted Riley to run it until Dave's return, or permanently if Trace bought it. Riley had just agreed to take over next week.

Now he could go see Jolene.

His stomach quivered with nerves as he mounted Baldy and headed out of town. The nearer he got to the Delaney farm, the faster his heart thumped. Then, when he got within sight of the house, it plummeted and almost quit beating altogether. An extra car sat in the driveway. Arthur Foley stood beside Jolene on the porch, their heads close together in deep discussion. Riley pulled Baldy to a halt in the road before either of them noticed him.

His gut felt as if he'd been kicked by a mule. He was too late. She had given up on him and found someone else.

Arthur had inherited his father's drugstore and owned a nice house. He had established himself as one of the town's leaders. A temporary job at the gas station paled in comparison. How could Riley hope to compete with Arthur?

Riley took a last hurried look at Jolene, enough to burn an image of her into his brain, and then gently wheeled the horse around and headed back to town.

Unsure where he was going, Riley kicked himself for turning around rather than riding on past the Delaney house to his own. He could go back to town and visit with Dave some more. Or he could go to the Chevrolet dealership and chat with Trace. He decided to go on to Trace's house and visit his sister.

"Why are you so depressed?" Callie asked after he told her about his new job. "You should be feeling good."

He shrugged. "I am."

"You don't look like you are." She removed Lily from his arms and sent her to play with her little brothers. Then she put her hands on Riley's shoulders and steered him down onto the sofa and sat beside him. She gazed into his face. "You got your life straight with God. You have a job lined up. Mom and Dad are thrilled to have you back here—and so am I. That leaves Jolene. Have you talked to her?"

Normally he would have given her a smack on the arm, or done something silly like tweaking her nose, and told her to stop being nosy and mind her own business. But he didn't.

"I meant to, but when I got in sight of her house I saw that she already had a caller."

Creases appeared between her brows. "Did you recognize him?"

He swallowed and forced the name past his lips. "Arthur Foley was on her front porch with her."

Callie's puzzled look cleared. "Ah, he must have been there on school business. He's president of the school board now, and the rural eighth graders are included in the town graduation."

As her explanation sank in, his heart rate increased. Hope began to swell in his chest. "Do you mean he's not courting her?"

A smirk crossed his sister's face. "He better not be. He married Nancy Perry a couple of years ago. Which is probably why he was conducting business on the open porch rather than going inside the house."

Riley sat there a moment, letting the facts he had just heard filter through his foggy brain.

Callie laughed. "Don't you have somewhere else you need to be?"

He picked up his hat and stood. She was right. He had to let Jolene know he loved her.

"Goodbye, Riley," she called as he spun and practically ran out the door.

Would Jolene accept his love? Could she still love him?

He climbed onto Baldy's back and set out, praying that God would touch her heart and cause her to look favorably on him.

The crisp March air no longer felt cool as Jolene worked in the garden. The exertion of pushing the hand plow forward, pulling back and pushing it forward again and again to dig a furrow in the ground had her dress sticking to her back.

After Arthur gave her the graduation plans and went over some smaller items discussed by the school board that would affect the rural schools, he had conveyed his regrets that they would not be able to increase her salary next year. But he had assured her that she still had a job if she wanted it.

"Jolene."

Intent on her plowing, the sound made her start and release the handles. As the plow toppled to the ground, she whirled—and nearly toppled with it. "Riley?"

Always lean and handsome, he had become more muscular—and looked so good. He wore denim pants, a pale blue shirt and a half smile. His eyes, dark and shiny beneath freshly trimmed black hair, moved over her, searching.

She squared her shoulders and folded her arms over her chest, fighting the urge to bolt. But pride rooted her feet to the ground. "Wh...what are you doing here?"

"I came to clear up a little matter," he said as he came to the edge of the garden plot. The slight curve of his mouth seemed tentative. "But I saw you working when I rode up and decided you need some help. I took this from your shed."

Jolene watched, transfixed, as he raised a length of rope and formed a loop at one end of it. Then he slipped his arms through it, secured it around his torso and went to the front of the plow. He set it upright and hooked the other end of the rope to the frame.

"Okay, let's get these rows plowed," he said, indicating she should take the handles.

Like an obedient child, she did as he instructed. As soon

as she had a firm grip, he turned and began to pull it while she pushed. At the end of the row, he moved the correct distance for another row, and they plowed their way back in the opposite direction. In far less time than it would have taken her to do it alone, they had neat rows all across that section of the garden, ready for onions, radishes and lettuce.

Riley worked the rope over his head and turned to face her.

Jolene pushed the plow to the edge of the plot and leaned it against a post of the fence that ran between the garden and the corral. When she released it, she felt uneasy at no longer having anything between them.

He watched her in silence. Then he took a step toward her. And stopped. His Adam's apple bobbed. Then he took another step. This time he didn't stop until they were face-to-face, his eyes locked on her.

"I got your letter," he said softly.

She blinked and reached out to touch his arm. "Oh, Riley."

He smiled, tenderness beaming down on her. "Trace and I talked."

"And?" she prompted when he paused, drowning in the black irises of his eyes.

"I made peace with God. I asked him to take over my life and forgive all the mistakes I've made. I'm free."

Joy began to seep through her, and then flared into full elation. Unable to restrain herself, Jolene wrapped her arms around him and pressed herself to his chest. When he responded by squeezing her so tightly she could hardly breathe, she sagged against him.

"I liked being looped to you."

His words in her ear made her look up. "Looped to me? Oh, you mean the plow," she whispered through a dry throat, the words airy and weak.

His face went totally serious. "I'd like to be hooked to you for life if you'll have me."

"You wa… You want…"

"To marry you."

Her jaw dropped.

"You once thought you loved me. Do you think you could again? I'll never be rich. I know I've hurt you in the past and made a lot of mistakes. I'm sorry for that. All I have to offer you is my love and a promise that I'll do everything in my power to take care of you. I…"

Joy bubbling up in her, Jolene blinked away tears and pressed a finger across his lips. "Riley, you don't have to convince me. I love you. I don't care if we'll never be rich. I don't care about your past. It made you the man you are, the man I love."

He pulled in a ragged breath and dipped his head to touch her lips in a kiss that made her knees go weak—and promised her the world.

"You'll marry me?" he asked when he eased back.

Her heart rejoiced as his rich, deep voice uttered the words she had longed to hear since her teens.

She reached up and gently caressed the side of his face. "Of course I'll marry you. All I need to make me happy is your love. I love you, Riley. I have for years. I want to be your wife and have a family with you."

When he leaned forward and touched his lips to hers again, she went up on tiptoe and slipped her arms around his neck. His arms tightened, and he kissed her soundly.

When he lifted his head, he tightened his arms around her some more and whirled her in a circle around the garden. When he finally set her down, he wore a satisfied grin. Then it disappeared. "Do you think your dad will let me have you?"

* * *

Sam faced Riley across the supper table Sunday evening.

"Son, I asked you to come back today and eat with us because I wanted to talk to you and Jolene while the Sullivan kids are visiting their aunt and uncle."

"Oops, I'm a kid." Irene shoved her chair back and moved to get up.

Sam held out a hand and pointed at the chair. "You stay right there, young lady. You might as well hear this. It will eventually affect you."

Uh-oh. This sounded ominous. Riley gulped. It helped when Jolene's hand clasped his beneath the table.

"As I said when you asked for Jolene's hand in marriage, I'm not opposed to you two getting married," Sam continued. "In fact, it's what I want. But I want to ask something of you. Will you live here until Irene is old enough to get married?"

"I'm old enough now," Irene blurted. "If I ever intended to get married. But I don't. I want to join a musical group and travel with them."

Sam's glare softened on his younger daughter. "You're old enough when I say so."

She gave him a cocky grin. "Which is when?"

"When you're out of school. As for your plans, I don't want to discourage you, but I guess you know that the gospel groups are mostly made up of men."

She shrugged. "I know. But that needs to change."

He heaved a long breath. "Go ahead and dream. But you'll get married."

He returned his attention to his older daughter and Riley, but he focused on Riley. "Now back to this proposal I have for you two. I've always planned to give each of the girls twenty acres of land when they marry. If you'll live here until Irene is out of school…" He paused to aim a pointed look at Irene. "You can have a house built by then."

Riley swallowed hard and took a quick breath. "I can't take your land, sir." As he said the words, unease tugged at his heart. Was his foolish pride making him refuse something that might be the right answer for them? What did Jolene want?

Sam rose and stepped to the cabinet at the side of the room. He reached up and took an envelope from the top of it and returned to the table. He placed it between them. "This is the deed to the section where Jolene told me years ago she would love to have a house of her own. I want you to have it."

Riley shook his head and started to refuse, but then he looked over at Jolene and read the longing in her eyes. "Is this what you want?" he asked softly.

"Only if you want it, too," she whispered back.

He studied her for several long moments, turning it over in his mind, and then turned back to face his future father-in-law.

"We'll accept it, sir. And I'll start on a house as soon as I help my parents finish theirs."

Sam cleared his throat. "I wouldn't have it any other way. Now I figure you two have better things to do than sit here with us."

"Yeah, get out of here," Irene ordered with a mischievous grin and a wave of her hand. "Dad will help me with the dishes. Won't you, Dad?"

Sam huffed. "Brat. Yes, I'll help."

Riley grabbed Jolene's hand, and they went to see what *better things* they could find to do.

Chapter 16

School dismissed for the summer on a Friday. The next afternoon Callie helped Jolene get ready. She smoothed the simple lines of the soft white dress they had made together and stepped back to survey it. "You look beautiful, and happy," she decreed, reaching out and squeezing Jolene's hands.

Jolene squeezed back. "I am. I love your brother, and we're going to be sisters. What more could I ask for?"

They hugged. When they parted, Callie escorted her outside. The sun shone bright and warm, the scent of new life filling the air. A bird's happy melody trilled from the trees that burst with brilliant new leaves. The day she had dreamed of for years was better than anything Jolene could have ordered.

Callie rode with Jolene and her dad to the church, her husband and kids having dropped her and gone on earlier. When they got there, the pews were packed. The sanctuary had been decorated with flowers and ribbons.

From the doorway Jolene peeked past Callie to where Riley and his brother, Delmer, who had come home from his WPA job to be his best man, stood. Looking utterly handsome, Riley wore a black suit and white shirt. But it was the warm look in his eyes locked on her that made Jolene's stomach do acrobatics. Along with the excitement came a surge of utter serenity.

When the "Wedding March" began, Callie started down the aisle. Then Jolene and her dad slowly followed her.

It was a simple wedding. Irene played the piano, and Jolene's students sang the song Irene had taught them.

When the pastor asked if she took Riley Blake to be her lawfully wedded husband, Jolene responded with an unhesitant, "I do." Her voice rang with confidence and love.

Riley's "I do" was deep and rich with sincerity.

The pastor pronounced them man and wife and announced, "You may kiss your bride."

Riley turned to face her and lifted her veil. A wide smile crossed his face, and a hand lifted to quiver against her face before he lowered his head and kissed her. "I love you," he whispered before he pulled back.

"And I love you," she whispered back.

United, they greeted the next chapter of their lives.

* * * * *

REQUEST YOUR FREE BOOKS!

2 FREE INSPIRATIONAL NOVELS
PLUS 2
FREE
MYSTERY GIFTS

Love Inspired®

LIDIR13R

REQUEST YOUR FREE BOOKS!

2 FREE INSPIRATIONAL NOVELS
PLUS 2
FREE
MYSTERY GIFTS

Love Inspired
HISTORICAL
INSPIRATIONAL HISTORICAL ROMANCE

YES! Please send me 2 FREE Love Inspired® Historical novels and my 2 FREE mystery gifts (gifts are worth about $10). After receiving them, if I don't wish to receive any more books, I can return the shipping statement marked "cancel." If I don't cancel, I will receive 4 brand-new novels every month and be billed just $4.74 per book in the U.S. or $5.24 per book in Canada. That's a savings of at least 21% off the cover price. It's quite a bargain! Shipping and handling is just 50¢ per book in the U.S. and 75¢ per book in Canada.* I understand that accepting the 2 free books and gifts places me under no obligation to buy anything. I can always return a shipment and cancel at any time. Even if I never buy another book, the two free books and gifts are mine to keep forever.

102/302 IDN F5CY

Name	(PLEASE PRINT)
Address	Apt. #
City	State/Prov.	Zip/Postal Code

Signature (if under 18, a parent or guardian must sign)

Mail to the Harlequin® Reader Service:
IN U.S.A.: P.O. Box 1867, Buffalo, NY 14240-1867
IN CANADA: P.O. Box 609, Fort Erie, Ontario L2A 5X3

Want to try two free books from another series?
Call 1-800-873-8635 or visit www.ReaderService.com.

* Terms and prices subject to change without notice. Prices do not include applicable taxes. Sales tax applicable in N.Y. Canadian residents will be charged applicable taxes. Offer not valid in Quebec. This offer is limited to one order per household. Not valid for current subscribers to Love Inspired Historical books. All orders subject to credit approval. Credit or debit balances in a customer's account(s) may be offset by any other outstanding balance owed by or to the customer. Please allow 4 to 6 weeks for delivery. Offer available while quantities last.

Your Privacy—The Harlequin® Reader Service is committed to protecting your privacy. Our Privacy Policy is available online at www.ReaderService.com or upon request from the Harlequin Reader Service.

We make a portion of our mailing list available to reputable third parties that offer products we believe may interest you. If you prefer that we not exchange your name with third parties, or if you wish to clarify or modify your communication preferences, please visit us at www.ReaderService.com/consumerschoice or write to us at Harlequin Reader Service Preference Service, P.O. Box 9062, Buffalo, NY 14269. Include your complete name and address.

LIHDIR13R